21% MONSTER

THE BOY WAS SLIGHTLY SHORT FOR A TWELVE-YEAR-OLD, BUT HE WAS AS BURLY AS A GROWN MAN. DESPITE HIS OBVIOUS STRENGTH AND THE NATURAL TOUGHNESS OF HIS BROAD FACIAL FEATURES, HE WATCHED MISS INGHART CAREFULLY, EVEN FEARFULLY.

THE IDEA THAT HE HAD DESTROYED AN ENTIRE BUILDING SEEMED IMPOSSIBLE.

For Mum and Dad

Thank you for believing I could write a book
despite all the evidence to the contrary.

First published in the UK in 2022 by Usborne Publishing Ltd., Usborne House,
83-85 Saffron Hill, London EC1N 8RT, England. www.usborne.com

Usborne Verlag, Usborne Publishing Ltd., Prüfeninger Str. 20, 93049 Regensburg,
Deutschland, VK Nr. 17560

Text copyright © P J Canning / Kickback Media Ltd, 2022

The right of P J Canning to be identified as the author
of this work has been asserted by him in accordance with the Copyright,
Designs and Patents Act, 1988.

The name Usborne and the Balloon logo are trade marks of Usborne Publishing Ltd.

A CIP catalogue record for this book is available from the British Library.

JFMA JJASOND/22 ISBN 9781474984416

Printed and bound in Great Britain by CPI Group (UK) Ltd, Croydon, CR0 4YY

MIX
Paper from
responsible sources
FSC® C171272

21%
MONSTER

P. J. CANNING

USBORNE

PROLOGUE

The body-cam video wobbled as the policeman ran, shouting, "Back from the van. Get back from the van!"

All around the car park, teenagers in blue blazers were huddled in groups. The officer ran between them, past a burning school building, towards a small group of kids who were being shepherded by a man away from the fire.

"Not towards the van, mate. AWAY FROM THE VAN!"

The wobbling body-cam image shifted from a boy, frozen in a moment of terror, and centred on the police van that the officer was sprinting towards. One of the back doors was hanging off its hinges, a twisted wreck, and inside some sort of struggle was going on. The officer jumped into the middle of the melee. The video lurched this way and that as an inhuman roar almost drowned out the cries of other officers.

"Calm down, now. Calm down!"

"Cuff him, quick!"

"You're okay, son, you're okay!"

Another roar erupted from the middle of the struggle.

"You need to look at me!" shouted the officer wearing the body cam. "I've got you, I've got you! Calm down! That's good, now just breathe. That's it…"

"Okay," another officer called out, her voice strained with effort. "'I've cuffed him!"

A blur of light-blue hair filled the body-cam picture as the officer broke away from the struggle. The video veered wildly, as the officer jumped clear of the van and then refocused on the wrecked vehicle. Inside sat a boy with his hands cuffed. His head was down, showing his blueish-blond hair, his extremely broad shoulders heaving as he breathed. He looked up, revealing a young, frightened face with amber-yellow eyes…

The video ended abruptly. Miss Inghart looked at the face staring out of her tablet, committing it to memory, and then glanced at Mr Ducas as he drove. "We have our target."

Ducas kept his eyes on the road and answered calmly in his distinctive North-Wales accent. "The video's on social media already?"

"Yes. Somebody leaked it. We don't have long."

"Farlington's two hours away."

"Make it ninety minutes," Miss Inghart answered.

"Copy that." Ducas glanced at her. "What are our orders?" he asked as he accelerated into the outside lane of the motorway, the car's hidden blue lights now flashing.

Miss Inghart quoted from the secure message she'd received: "Identify whether the target is of interest. If he is, complete a Triple E operation."

Ducas nodded. "Okay. Do we have info on the target yet? Name? Age?"

"Coming through now..." Miss Inghart read the information and grimaced. "His name is Darren Devlin. He's twelve years old."

Ducas raised an eyebrow as he squeezed his way through traffic at high speed. "They've confirmed this is Triple E?"

"Affirmative," Miss Inghart replied. "Extract. Evaluate. Eliminate."

CHAPTER 1

EXPECTATIONS

Twenty-four hours earlier…

The football slammed into the wall just ahead of Darren. The Year Eleven boys laughed. Darren lowered his head and kept walking. The ball flew past him again, this time brushing his leg. The boys laughed louder. Darren felt anger rise inside him. He stopped and turned.

Alexander Harrison stood grinning, spinning the ball between his hands. He nodded towards the main school block. "Well, go on then, loser. You don't want to be late for weirdo class."

Darren hesitated and then walked on. He heard the dull thud of Alexander kicking the ball again. Instinctively, he turned and caught it just centimetres from his face.

"Oooh!" the Year Eleven boys jeered, their eyes drifting from Alexander to Darren, who stared up at them defiantly.

Most of them were at least a head taller than him. He looked around. The last few pupils were leaving the schoolyard for afternoon lessons and there were no teachers in sight.

Alexander reached out a hand. "Give me the ball."

Darren didn't move.

"Come on! We were kidding around. We're done now." The bell for lessons rang. "Hear that?" Alexander asked. "We've all got lessons, right? Come on, where's your sense of humour?"

Darren watched Alexander's face, all fake-reasonable against a background of grinning boys. Anger bubbled inside him as his eyes drifted to the ball. He placed a hard-nailed thumb against either side of the ball and squeezed until he felt them sink through the outer lining. He stared defiantly at Alexander as the ball punctured with a dull pop.

Alexander's mouth fell open as he watched the ball deflate with a loud hiss. "Why, you little—"

Darren didn't wait to find out what Alexander called him. He ran around the corner of the swimming pool building, throwing the ball back at his pursuers, and dodged through a maintenance door. He raced into the boiler room and began to climb a wall as running footsteps drew near. He clambered through the large pipes that criss-crossed the ceiling and pulled his legs up until he was fully hidden. Below him, Alexander burst into view.

"Where are you, you little freak?" he yelled.

Darren watched the top of Alexander's head as the older boy moved through the boiler room beneath him. He held his breath as Alexander stopped and listened. Through the wall, he heard footsteps. The boiler-room door flew open.

"Hey, Alexander!"

Darren grinned at the familiar voice of his big sister.

"What, Daisy?" Alexander shouted.

"You should be in lessons. The boiler room is out of bounds."

"Walk away, Daisy. This has got nothing to do with you. Believe me, you want to keep it that way!"

"Miss Fredricks is out here. Shall I call her over?" Daisy asked sweetly.

Alexander hestitated and then ran out of the room. Darren exhaled slowly with relief.

"Darren, are you in there?" Daisy called from outside. When Darren didn't answer, she added, "I have to go. You need to get to class!"

He listened to her jog away and felt guilty for not responding, but coming down would mean facing Alexander Harrison after school at the main gate. He decided to stay put and rested his head against a water pipe. The slow, steady gurgle of the water soothed him, reminding him of breathing. He shut his eyes and let the warmth and rhythm take him somewhere dark. Somewhere safe. Somewhere far away from the school he hated so much.

Darren woke with a start. From the ache in his shoulders, he guessed he'd been asleep for hours. He swung down from the pipe, dropped to the floor and listened. Outside seemed quiet. He opened the boiler-room door and groaned when he saw the setting sun.

The schoolyard was empty and the buildings were mostly dark as he made his way towards the main entrance, wondering what time it was. If he was lucky, he could catch a bus and get home before his mum and dad. He ran as far as the car park – but then skidded to a halt as he spotted his mum's car parked in front of the school.

His stomach churned as he turned and trudged towards the headmistress's office, already imagining the look of disappointment on his mum's face. The headmistress's light was on, so Darren drifted past her window and hid safely in the shadows.

Her voice floated out of the window. "Mrs Devlin, Darren disappeared again today – for the whole afternoon."

Darren heard his mum answer. "I'm so sorry, Mrs Carver!"

"This is not the first time he's vanished during the school day."

"We've talked to him about it. We really have."

"As have we. We will also have to speak to him about destruction of property. He deliberately damaged a Year Eleven boy's football today."

"What? I'm so sorry, I really am… I don't know what to say!"

Darren gritted his teeth at the embarrassed tone in his mum's voice.

Mrs Carver sighed. "That's the problem, Mrs Devlin, neither do I. It's not just his behaviour outside class that worries me, either. Darren won't speak up in lessons, and I'm told he often actually *hides* under his desk. He has made absolutely no progress with his reading, even now he's working alone with a teaching assistant. He doesn't seem to want to try reading at all—"

His mum interrupted, the pitch of her voice rising. "But you knew that. You knew all of this when you agreed to teach him here. You said St Bartle's was the perfect school for him! You said the school was ideal for someone with special educational needs."

Mrs Carver chose her words carefully. "I did. I did say that. We are a small school, Mrs Devlin – parents pay a lot of money to send their children here – and we are able to give special help to pupils who struggle, in a way that state schools cannot. I have, however, never before had a student who makes no progress at all—"

His mum interrupted. "So maybe you were arrogant? We told you how serious his reading problem is and you said 'Don't worry'!"

Mrs Carver's tone hardened. "Nevertheless, you have to understand that all this puts me in a difficult position."

"I don't understand."

"Mrs Devlin, Darren destroyed property today. I've had a complaint from a parent. Each time he goes missing, staff have to look for him. I can't justify Darren's place at this school if he chooses to make no effort. I'm afraid my next option will be to exclude him permanently."

"You're throwing him out? No. No! When you offered Daisy her scholarship, we told you about Darren. We told you we couldn't have them in different schools. You said you'd take him. You said you'd help him. You *promised!*"

"Mrs Devlin, this is out of my hands. If Darren breaks school rules once more, he is out."

"If Darren leaves, then so does Daisy," his mum shouted. "Do you understand? You won't get to brag about her perfect grades after the summer!"

Darren heard the door slam.

* * *

By the time his mum reached the car, Darren was standing by the passenger door.

"Sorry, Mum."

She sighed. "Get in."

He watched his mum's troubled expression as they drove in silence. Her dark-blue nurse's uniform was creased and she'd pegged her dark hair up in a messy bun with a pencil, the way she always did when she was tired from a long shift. He felt bad for giving her something to worry about when she should be resting. She opened her mouth to speak as she slowed for a red traffic light.

Darren saved her the trouble. "Mum, I heard."

She glanced at him as the lights changed. "Okay." She gripped his hand tightly until she had to change gear. "I'll explain to your dad."

Darren didn't answer, but instead gazed out of the window at the passing hedgerows.

His dad's car was in the drive when they got home. Darren disappeared to his room and changed into jeans and a T-shirt featuring *The Clash,* his favourite punk band, before he got the call to come down for dinner. He chased a chicken salad around his plate, quietly watching his parents' subdued conversation with Daisy about her day. She glanced worriedly between the three of them as they all ate, and then volunteered to wash up, leaving Darren alone with his parents. He looked between his mum and dad, wondering who would speak first.

His dad looked at him. "Darren, Mum explained about today. You know what your head teacher said."

"I'm sorry."

"That's the thing, Darren. You're always sorry, but it keeps happening."

Darren looked down to avoid his dad's eyes.

His dad ran a hand through his thinning blond hair and adjusted his glasses before continuing. "We know how hard you find school, we really do. And we love you. You know that?"

Darren nodded, and risked a fleeting look at his parents. His dad seemed exhausted while his mum's eyes were tearing up. He looked down again. "Yeah, I do."

"It's just…" His dad hesitated. "You need to be more…"

Darren looked up. *Go on, say it*, he thought to himself. *Say what you want to say.*

"Son, you need to be more aware of people's expectations."

Darren sank lower in his chair. "Okay."

"You're twelve now. It's up to you."

"Yeah, I know. I'm sorry."

They sat in silence for a moment that drifted into an eternity.

"Off you go," his dad said eventually.

Darren went up to his room and switched on his music, playing the loudest punk song he could find. Under the cover of the noise, he opened his bedroom window and climbed out onto the sill, closing the window behind him. Ignoring the sound of passing cars and the occasional bark of a neighbourhood dog, he tuned in to the quiet of the night: the rhythm of the autumn wind blowing through the trees behind the garden fence and the calls of animals waking from the slumber of the day; the evening's first bats swooping to catch fluttering moths while birds roosted. He clambered down the drainpipe and, checking that his mum wasn't at the window, vaulted over the back fence into the woods beyond.

The darkness was complete. Darren stood, feeling himself relax in the safety of the blackness. A long, thick branch of his favourite sycamore stretched down to him like the arm of an old friend, and he leaped up, grabbed it and climbed until he could see the town of Farlington to the east and Old River Road to the west. The town seemed darker and uglier than usual. The ancient bridge and old market square were mainly hidden from view by the sprawl of newer buildings and roads that stretched to their estate on the edge of town. He looked out at the peacefulness of the river beyond the old road and imagined swimming upstream to faraway mountains he had never seen. Maybe up there he could find a quiet cave where he'd never have to worry about people's expectations again.

"Tiny?" Being petite like her mother, Daisy had to stand on tiptoe to look over the fence. She called him by the nickname she'd used since he was a toddler. "Tiny?"

"Yeah, Daisy?"

"Help me over."

Darren clambered down and extended a hand from an overhanging branch.

Daisy pulled herself up and sat beside him in the almost total darkness. "I still don't know how you can climb like that."

"Do you want to go higher?"

"Sure," she answered and swung her arms around his neck. Darren climbed back up until he found a branch big enough for both of them, with a view of the river. "It's beautiful," she said.

"Yeah."

She nudged him. "Is it true you ripped up Alexander's ball?"

He grinned. "I only stuck my thumbs in."

"What was his face like?"

Darren mimicked Alexander's gormless open mouth.

Daisy laughed. "He deserved it."

"Maybe," Darren answered glumly. "I got angry. I don't like it when I get angry."

"What did Dad say?"

"I need to be more aware of people's expectations."

Daisy looked unimpressed. "What are you supposed to do with that?"

"Doesn't matter. It's not what he meant."

Daisy looked concerned. "What do you think he meant?"

"I need to be more normal."

Daisy put an arm as far around his shoulders as she could manage. "Don't say that! He's never said that! He loves you, you know."

"Okay."

"I mean it!"

"Okay," Darren answered again, even though he knew exactly what his dad had been thinking. He looked out over the river. "The school are going to chuck me out."

"They can't do that!"

"I do one more thing wrong and I'm out. That's what they said."

"Then I leave too," Daisy said defiantly.

"No."

"Yes."

Darren sighed. "It's your GCSEs soon. You've got to stay. You're clever. That school is right for you. Plus they help with your dancing, like getting you into that competition tomorrow."

"You're more important."

I'm not, Darren thought. *Dad knows I'm not and I know he's right.* He shook his head. "That school gets people into Oxfart University and places like that."

Daisy rolled her eyes. "*Oxford* University."

"Whatever. You're good enough to get there. Or that royal dance place."

"You're my little brother, Tiny. It won't mean anything without you being okay at school."

Darren looked her in the eye. "It would to me." He ran a hand from the top of his head to the top of hers, hardly having to raise it. "And I'm not so tiny any more."

"Okay." There was a tinge of sadness in her voice. "But I'm always going to call you Tiny, you know? I always will."

Darren grinned. "Yeah, and every time I'm in trouble, you warn me I've got a 'Tiny problem'. I know."

Daisy tipped her head and looked at him closely. "Wish me luck for tomorrow?" She extended a fist towards him.

Darren clenched his fist and gently bumped his sister's. His hand was far larger than hers. "Good luck."

"I'm going to be worrying about you."

"Don't." Darren looked at his sister and sighed. "It's only one day, right?"

"Just keep a low profile, okay?" she said.

Darren smiled. "I can do that." He sniffed the shifting breeze. "We'd better go in. Rain's coming."

Daisy held on tight again as her brother clambered down. "You're more amazing than any of them," she whispered in his ear.

"Keep thinking that," Darren answered, as he landed and carefully lifted her over the fence; then added in his own mind, *Even if you're the only one who does, Daisy.*

Later, Darren lay wrapped in his duvet under his bed as the night inched by and heavy rain lashed the window. He felt more awake than he had all day as he stuck in his earbuds and played his favourite bands. He listened to Johnny Rotten ranting his way through a song and wondered if anyone had ever had to speak to him about other people's expectations.

The day ahead loomed ominously and anger bubbled deep inside as he thought about Mrs Carver, Alexander Harrison and all the rest of them. It crept through his veins, filling him with a strange and powerful nervous energy. He breathed out and pushed the anger down, forcing himself to relax. In the dark safety of the familiar space under his bed, he could let himself admit that he feared the anger inside him more than anything in the world outside.

His anger was more than just a feeling. It was like it had a personality of its own. A destructive genie he had to keep firmly in the bottle.

CHAPTER 2

A WISE DECISION

Miss Inghart looked up from her phone as Ducas rounded a bend, drove towards the school and slowed down. Groups of people were standing randomly in the road and on the pavements. Miss Inghart watched as parents comforted their children and tearful teenagers hugged each other. Ducas drove past a line of TV news crews and pulled up at the blue-and-white tape of a police cordon.

"Who are we today, Miss Inghart?" Ducas asked.

"Serious Crime Squad."

Ducas took an ID card from Miss Inghart and held it up as a policeman approached the driver's window. "Scotland Yard Serious Crime," he said as he passed the ID to the officer.

"Afternoon, Inspector. I didn't realize we'd gone national with this."

"Is the suspect still here, Constable?"

The policeman shook his head. "No, sir. He's at the station. Never seen anything like it. He actually ripped a hole in the van door. The station's not far – just back up, take the road past the school and then the first left."

Ducas did as instructed and gave a slow whistle as he drove on. "He flattened that building?"

Miss Inghart didn't respond as she looked at the rubble of St Bartle's School. Smoke drifted across the scene. A single fire engine sent a spray of water onto what remained of the main building.

Ducas turned a corner and drove away from the school towards the police station. "They're really saying one person did all that?"

Miss Inghart nodded and then pulled her long blonde hair into a tight, professional-looking ponytail. "The social media reports are remarkably consistent."

They pulled up at the station beside a police van. There was a jagged hole ripped in one back door; the other was hanging off its hinges.

"You still want to go in alone?" Ducas asked.

"It's better that way."

"I'd like you to be armed."

Miss Inghart tapped her trouser leg. "Pepper spray."

Ducas shook his head. "Join me at the back of the car."

Miss Inghart scanned the surrounding area while Ducas opened the car boot and lifted a false floor. Inside a hidden compartment were two pistols, a sub-machine gun, a dart rifle and a stun gun.

He lifted the stun gun. "Just in case?"

Miss Inghart checked to see that the car park was still deserted, then nodded and put the gun in her briefcase.

"I doubt that'll stun him for long if we're right," Ducas said, "so you might need to get out in a hurry."

"I'm sure I can deal with him. I want you back up at the school. See what you can find out."

Ducas nodded. "Okay. Keep the car." He took a pistol from the boot, put it in a holster under his suit jacket and then jogged out of sight. Miss Inghart shut the boot and took a moment to compose herself before walking into the station. She approached the desk sergeant, holding up her ID as she did so.

"Hello, I'm Dr Wiseman. Psychologist with Scotland Yard. Have you seen it up there at the school? He really did all that alone?"

"That's what they're saying," the sergeant answered. He looked flustered.

"I'd like to see him."

"Not sure that's a good idea, seeing what he did to the van—"

She interrupted him. "I'll be fine."

"Shouldn't we wait for his lawyer?"

"I'm just assessing him."

The sergeant scratched the back of his neck. "I don't know…"

Miss Inghart smiled. "I understand. Why don't you ring Scotland Yard? They want a psychologist's report on the suspect ASAP." She handed him her ID. "The number's there."

"Okay." The sergeant picked up his phone.

"Ask for Department Ten."

The sergeant nodded. "Hello. Department Ten, please… Farlington police station. Yes, yes…surprising day. Thank you." He motioned to Miss Inghart that he was on hold. "Hello? Yes, I have a Dr Wiseman here. She wants…" The sergeant listened to whoever was speaking, then the colour drained from his face. He looked at Miss Inghart and slowly put the phone down. "Tell you what, why don't you just go on ahead? I'll buzz you through."

Miss Inghart smiled again. "Thank you!"

She walked down the hall and peered through the interview-room window. The suspect was sitting quietly, a pair of broken handcuffs on the table in front of him. She nodded to the constable on guard duty, who unlocked the door. She knocked before entering.

"Darren?" she said quietly. "Can I speak to you?"

He looked at her. Two piercing amber-yellow eyes under a shock of wild hair. Under the electric lights, his hair colour was hard to pin down. One moment it seemed blond, and the next, tinted blue.

"My name is Anne. Dr Anne Wiseman. Can I speak to you? Please?"

The boy was slightly short for a twelve-year-old, but he was as burly as a grown man. Despite his obvious strength and the natural toughness of his broad facial features, he watched Miss Inghart carefully, even fearfully. He seemed much younger than twelve years old. The idea that he had destroyed an entire building seemed impossible.

Miss Inghart passed him a bottle of water from her briefcase as she sat down opposite him. "You must be thirsty."

Darren hesitantly took the bottle and sipped. "Thanks." They sat watching each other.

Miss Inghart finally broke the silence, keeping her voice soft. "Can you tell me what happened?"

Darren frowned. "Some kids were after me. I remember trying to hide. That's all."

"Are you good at hiding?"

"The best," Darren answered.

"Do you hide a lot at school?"

Darren nodded.

"The other children aren't nice to you?"

Darren tipped his head. Half a shake and half a nod.

"Where's your best hiding place?"

Darren took his time answering. "The swimming pool."

Miss Inghart smiled. Darren smiled back. She leaned forward. He shifted his weight, moving a little further away.

"I'm not going to hurt you, Darren. Where do you hide at the pool? The changing rooms?"

Darren shook his head.

"They'd guess that, I suppose? Where else is there to hide?"

"The boiler room, up in the pipes or in the water."

"Under the water?"

Darren nodded. "Bottom of the deep end. They never look there."

"How long do you stay under the water?"

"All through break sometimes."

"Fifteen minutes? Really?"

Darren nodded and blushed.

"You couldn't hide today?"

"Pool was closed."

"So what did you do?"

"I tried shouting. That usually scares them off."

"Are you loud when you shout, Darren?"

Darren drank the remaining water in one gulp before he answered. "The loudest."

Miss Inghart smiled. "Because you don't want to fight."

"I don't like fighting."

"But today they didn't get scared off. Am I right?"

Darren nodded. "They were, like, sixteen years old. My sister usually stops the Year Elevens." Darren's expression brightened for a moment when he mentioned his sister, and then darkened again. "But she was away today...with Mum and Dad."

"You love your sister?"

He smiled. "Yeah."

"So today Year Elevens came after you. There was nowhere to hide and shouting didn't work. They hit you?"

Darren nodded. "I punctured their football yesterday. They wanted payback."

"And you fought back?"

Darren looked down and then glanced worriedly at her. "I don't remember."

"Are you sure, Darren?"

A note of frustration entered his voice. "I don't remember anything!"

"Okay," she answered. "Don't worry."

Darren looked around him.

"Something wrong, Darren?"

"Can you hear that sound? *Wee-wee-wah-wah*. Really annoying."

A dog howled in the distance. Miss Inghart smiled. "No, but it sounds like the dog heard it too."

Darren looked down again. "Am I in trouble at school?" he asked. "They were going to chuck me out."

She nodded sympathetically. "I'm afraid so, Darren. A lot of trouble. Worse than being excluded."

Darren shifted uneasily. "What did I do?"

"You destroyed the main building," Miss Inghart answered, and watched Darren struggle to process the news. *He really didn't know*, she thought to herself, *but it doesn't surprise him either*.

He looked at her, his yellow eyes wide with worry. "Am I going to prison?"

Miss Inghart leaned closer and this time Darren didn't back away. "I expect they'll want to put you in juvenile detention. Do you know what that is?"

Darren's gaze dropped to the floor. "Prison for kids."

Miss Inghart whispered, "You know you're different, don't you?"

Darren stared at her and then nodded cautiously.

Miss Inghart smiled. "I think, maybe, you are very special. Now, we don't have to talk about this any more. Why don't you tell me a bit about your family?"

They talked for a while, Miss Inghart mentally noting small details on how Darren talked about himself and his life, until she heard two police cars arrive outside. She leaned forward and spoke urgently. "Darren, listen to me. The police and the judges will want to lock you away for the rest of your life, but I think you just need help from some special people I know."

Darren looked hopeful. "Really?"

"Yes." Miss Inghart patted his arm. "I have to go now, Darren. Be good for the police. Can you do that? Just remember I'm on your side and wherever they take you, I'll find you and help."

Darren nodded and gave half a smile. "Okay."

Miss Inghart got up, put the empty water bottle in her briefcase and slipped out of the door. She looked at Darren through the window for a moment, as he rubbed his arm thoughtfully on the place where she had touched it, and then strode away.

Ducas jogged down the hill a few minutes after Miss Inghart got back to the car.

"What did you find out?" she asked.

"He totally flattened the main block and took part of a wall out of another one. The pupils and teachers hid in a cellar or ran for it, though one kid called Alexander Harrison's been found screaming his head off, hanging by his belt from a lamp post – they're still getting him down. Seems the lad did it all on his own. He's not very academic, a loner who's been in trouble a lot. He goes missing for hours at a time and then just turns up – that kind of thing."

"Family?"

"Out of town at a dance competition and due back in an hour. The family is pretty normal. The father, Brian Devlin, is a paramedic. The mother, Lily Devlin, is a nurse. His sister, Daisy, is a bit of a high-flyer. She's on an academic scholarship, talented dancer, intelligent, captain of a couple of sports teams. Due to be Head Girl. She looks out for him…"

"But she wasn't at school today," Miss Inghart finished. "High-flyer, huh? Funny how life rolls the dice."

"Hilarious," Ducas answered without cracking a smile as he replaced their weapons in the hidden compartment. "What did you get out of the boy? Is he what we think he might be?"

Miss Inghart held up the water bottle. "I think so. The truth drug got him talking. He can hear outside the normal human range. He can hold his breath for a really long time…and he really does have blue hair when the light catches it. I've got his DNA on the bottle too, so we'll know by tomorrow."

Ducas shut the boot. His dark eyes scanned her face for a reaction. "Blue hair?"

Miss Inghart let a trace of excitement into her voice. "I know."

He stayed impassive as he considered the information. "Okay. You want me to extract him now? I have enough tranquillizers to knock out an elephant in here. We could have him at HQ before he wakes up."

Miss Inghart shook her head. "No. I'll submit a report saying the boy's criminally insane. I'll say he must be kept away from everyone, including his family. They'll stick him in a high-security juvenile prison."

"Well, it's your decision, but it sounds a lot more complicated than elephant tranqs."

"I want to make sure that when we break him out of prison he thinks we're the good guys."

Ducas raised a cynical eyebrow. "I thought we *were* the good guys."

Miss Inghart smiled. "Sometimes you Brits have a funny sense of humour. You drive. I need to call HQ."

As they drove away, a tall thin boy appeared beside a tree as if from nowhere. His face was obscured by a broad-brimmed hat pulled down low and a pair of sunglasses, but what little skin was visible was incredibly pale. He walked over to the police van and inspected the damage to the doors. Crouching, he pulled a pair of tweezers from the jacket pocket of his dark suit and lifted up a single long blue hair.

His small mouth broke into a smile.

CHAPTER 3

YOU CAN'T HIDE FOREVER

Miss Inghart sat opposite Mr and Mrs Devlin in their small, tidy living room. She chose her words carefully. "I realize this is hard to understand—"

Mrs Devlin interrupted. "Dr Wiseman, I understand completely, but I'm Darren's mother! How you describe him…well, it just isn't the boy I know. He's a good boy. A sweet boy. He's never got into fights!"

Miss Inghart placed the cup of tea Mrs Devlin had given her on the floor, quietly wondering how the British could drink the stuff. She spoke sympathetically. "I meant it's hard emotionally." She turned to Mr Devlin who had been quiet so far. With his thin body and neat blond hair, it was hard to see a resemblance to his son until you looked closely, but there was something in the shape of his eyes maybe.

"Mr Devlin, your son is very disturbed. At the moment, he's violent. He needs to be isolated. In a place that's safe for him."

"At Bleakmoor Prison!" Mrs Devlin answered angrily. Mr Devlin stayed quiet.

Miss Inghart nodded to show she understood her concerns. "I may be able to help him, but first he needs to be safe and other people need to be safe from him."

"No!"

"Mrs Devlin—"

"NO!" she shouted. "This is just like the school not understanding him or those doctors who kept trying to test his eyes just because they are such a rare colour even though he can see incredibly well. Everyone wants to make Darren a problem and focus on what's different about him, but he deserves more than that. He always has and I won't let you take him, just like I never let the doctors run him through a million tests for no reason! He's a boy. He's our son and we'll help him. No one else!"

"Lily, please, let her finish." Mr Devlin gripped his wife's hand.

Miss Inghart continued. "I am probably the one person who stands between your son and a lifetime in prison. He needs to be separated from everything he knows. Please let me help him."

Mrs Devlin opened her mouth to shout again, but Mr Devlin stopped her, addressing Miss Inghart. "Can you give us a minute?"

"Of course." Miss Inghart left the room and listened from the hallway to the whispered argument as Mr Devlin slowly persuaded his wife to let their son go. She smiled to herself and moved away to make a phone call.

"Mr Ducas?" she said in a low voice.

"*Here.*"

"It's sorted. They'll be moving him to Bleakmoor tomorrow morning. Can you get a chemical tracker in his food before he's moved?"

"*Done,*" Ducas replied. "*How long do we wait to extract?*"

"At least a few days. He needs to think his family have abandoned him. Then we rescue him."

"*Okay, I'll prepare an extraction plan.*"

Miss Inghart cut the call and forced a sombre expression onto her face. She knocked on the door to the front room and went back in – without ever noticing that the kitchen door was ajar and that Daisy had been listening behind it.

Darren jumped, gripped the bars on his cell window and looked at the drizzle-filled grey sky that stretched out into the distance. Below him, the dark stone walls of Bleakmoor

High-Security Prison did nothing to make the view more appealing.

He dropped back down and rested his head against the cell wall. The chill of the cold stone crept through him and a sense of despair followed. Five days ago, at this time in the evening, he'd been sitting in a tree with Daisy, worrying about being excluded from school. Now, he was facing a life in this cold, forbidding building out in the middle of nowhere. And from past experience, he felt sure the other boys here weren't going to like him at all.

His thoughts drifted to his family and a huge sense of guilt gripped him to add to the despair. He hadn't kept the genie in the bottle and now everything was ruined. *This is all my fault,* he thought to himself, and punched the wall.

Footsteps rang out as someone walked along the metal gangway outside the row of cells. They were heavy enough to be a guard's feet. Darren sat on the edge of the bed – *his* bed now – and waited.

The door opened. "Come on, lad. You can't stay in here for ever." It was Mr Styles, who had brought him into the prison on his first day. "The best way to deal with this place is to meet the other boys."

"I want to see my mum and dad. I want to see my sister." It was all Darren could think to say.

"Sorry, lad. It's like they told you. You're too high-risk. No visitors for now."

Darren felt a hole open up inside him. "Can I call them?"

Mr Styles seemed to lose patience. "Listen, lad. This is an order. Get down those stairs!" He turned and left the cell.

Darren didn't know how far Bleakmoor was from home, but it felt like a million miles. He padded over to the door and peered out at the hall below. At one end, some teenagers were playing pool. At the other, a large group were watching TV. He took a deep breath and walked out, his trainers making a loud thudding noise as he slowly headed down the metal stairs. A couple of boys near the TV looked up, their expressions hard to read.

Darren made for a chair by the teenagers playing pool and sat down without looking at anyone.

"See that, Harry?" a boy said as he potted a ball. "The new kid is sitting on one of our chairs."

Darren froze.

"I do, Chris. You see that, Ahmed? Josh?"

"Yeah."

"Yeah."

Harry whistled. "Hey, kid. What's with the blue hair?"

Darren looked up. "It's blond. Electric lights make it look blue."

Harry laughed. "Your mum tell you that?"

Darren blushed and ran his hand through his wild hair.

Chris grinned. "Do the lights make your eyes look yellow too?"

Darren shrugged.

"First time behind bars?"

The question sounded polite, but all four teenagers stared as they waited for an answer. The group had a menace about them that made Alexander Harrison and his cronies seem like pussycats by comparison.

Darren didn't respond. He looked over at the only other boy nearby, who was also sitting in a chair by the pool table. Darren was sure this boy hadn't been there when he'd sat down. He was wearing a suit, unlike the orange tracksuits all the other boys had to wear on the high-security wing, and was texting. Darren frowned – he'd been told phones weren't allowed in the detention centre, and neither were your own clothes.

The teenagers followed Darren's gaze, but didn't seem to see the boy, who looked up, nodded politely to Darren and then returned to his phone. Darren glanced at the pool-playing teenagers and then back at the boy they couldn't seem to see.

"What you in for?" Chris asked. "Stealing?"

Darren blushed with shame. "I smashed up my school."

"Oh, you're *that* boy! They say you properly flattened it! Did you use a bulldozer?"

Darren looked down. He couldn't remember, but somehow he knew he'd only used his bare hands.

"You going to answer?" Harry asked.

Darren kept his gaze on his hands, then he got up and walked away. Hearing footsteps following him, he ducked into the toilets. The door banged open behind him.

Harry laughed. "Where d'you think you're going?"

Darren turned to see the four teenagers spreading out, tapping the floor with their pool cues.

Chris stepped close. "Nobody sits in our chairs."

"I didn't know."

Chris shrugged. "We know. Problem is, the other boys will wonder why we let a short, wide, blue-haired, yellow-eyed freak like you get away with it."

Darren's heart was beating hard. He knew what was coming. The boys slammed their cues on the cubicle doors with a steady rhythm as they chanted, "Freak, freak, freak!"

Chris raised his pool cue, ready to strike.

The muscles in Darren's back tightened. He felt anger mixing with his fear.

"Freak, freak, freak!"

Darren flexed his shovel-like hands. His hair stood on end as his anger swelled. They weren't going to call him

41

a freak. They'd done that at school. Now it was a pile of rubble.

"I'm not a frea—OAARRRR!!!!" His bones vibrated as his shout became a deep roar. The teenagers dropped their cues and fled screaming, leaving the door swinging behind them.

Darren's anger ebbed away and he breathed deeply. Cautiously, he left the toilets. The pool-table gang were nowhere to be seen, but his stomach twisted as a crowd of boys moved away from the TV towards him. Avoiding their gazes, he ran for the stairs and swung his way up, using the banisters as much as the steps. He sprinted into his cell and dived under the bed. The shadows wrapped around him, keeping him safe, just as they did every night at home. He curled into a ball and watched a spider spin its web.

"If they want me to come out, they'll have to drag me!" he whispered.

The evening turned into night as Darren lay still. Hardly daring to breathe, he wondered if Dr Wiseman would keep her promise to help him.

A single set of footsteps. Two perfectly polished black shoes came into view, each beneath a neatly ironed trouser leg. Darren curled up tighter.

"Most odd…" said a calm voice.

One leg kneeled and a head came into view, looking at Darren in his hiding place. He recognized the boy who had been sitting by the pool table. Up close, Darren saw that he looked very strange. As well as being extremely tall and thin, his forehead was high and domed and his dark hair was so sparse that his pale skin showed clearly through it. His eyes were oval-shaped with unusually large black irises.

The boy blinked once, his eyelids closing at an odd angle, making a V-shape that matched his curious frown, and then said, more to himself than to Darren, "Fascinating! I imagine you sleep under the bed even when you're at home."

Darren stayed quiet, wondering how he'd guessed that.

The boy stood up. "Perhaps I can make this room more hospitable." The lights switched off and the door closed. "Would you mind coming out from under there? I'm guessing the darkness helps. I broke into prison to help you, not hurt you."

Darren rolled out of his hiding place and stood. He was much shorter and far broader than his unexpected visitor, and he looked up warily into the boy's face, which was lit only by the light from his phone.

"How'd you turn the lights off and shut the door? Only the guards can do that."

The boy waved his phone. "Technology is easy to manipulate when you know how, but that's an odd question to start with. Asking why I'm here might be better." He extended a hand. "Or you could ask my name. How do you do? I'm Marek Masters."

Darren shook his hand. "Darren Devlin."

There was something odd about Marek's grip. Darren saw that his hand had three very long fingers and two almost equally long thumbs. One thumb was where Darren would have expected to see a little finger.

Marek smiled. "I'm excited to meet you."

Darren watched him closely. If Marek was excited, he was hiding it well.

Marek watched him back. "I imagine you have other questions?"

"Umm… Why couldn't the others see you?"

Marek shrugged. "A simple hypnofield. It's a skill I inherited from the more talented part of my family. Human minds are easily fooled."

Darren frowned. "But I saw you."

"Yes, but you're different!"

"I'm not a freak," Darren answered defensively.

"Did I say you were? Let's just say you have interesting talents and being resistant to hypnotism seems to be one of them."

"No, let's not."

Marek regarded him thoughtfully. "There are things I've found out. Things I think you should know. I'd appreciate it if you'd listen."

Darren shifted uneasily, then sat on his bunk. "All right, I'm all ears."

Marek tapped a finger to one of his incredibly tiny ears. "These are a touchy subject."

"Sorry."

"Forgiven." Marek cleared his throat. "The story begins fifteen or sixteen years ago. A secret organization, working within governments and major corporations, decided that the people of this country and its allies were letting them down. They thought the people were neither intelligent enough nor tough enough to compete in the modern world. So they set up a project to see if they could 'improve' the DNA of the next generation. They called it *Project Helix*. They created a synthetic virus that could add new DNA to human DNA. Are you following me so far?"

"Yeah, kind of," Darren answered.

"Good. To begin Project Helix, they picked three primary schools in the poorest neighbourhoods they could find in Britain, Poland and the United States. They placed undercover agents into each school as teachers, and doctors into the local surgeries and hospitals. They even moved their people into the chosen neighbourhoods as shop owners or supposedly normal families.

"Then they began the experiment: small local tests to see what would happen, with a plan to repeat it on a huge scale if it worked. The virus was put into school dinners, given to all of the children every school day. No one discovered its existence because the virus forms inside the human body, plants the DNA and then immediately breaks apart again. It is almost impossible to detect." Marek smiled knowingly. "Almost."

"That's terrible!"

Marek nodded. "They used two kinds of genetic material. One from a creature more intelligent than humans. The other came from, well...something truly fearsome, it seems."

"What happened?"

Marek continued. "They slowly increased the average dose of the virus over months and months for several years. They looked at school test results and checked medical records. They watched and waited, but the experiment failed. In the early years, they found nothing. Then, the very moment they started to see changes in intelligence or behaviour in a small number of the nine hundred and thirty children who were given the virus, those few children started to get sick. Really, really sick. Forty-nine children, and none of them ever recovered."

"They died?" Darren asked, shocked.

Marek nodded gravely. "Faced with the possibility of hundreds of unexplained deaths that could expose the experiment, Project Helix was abandoned thirteen years ago. They blamed the deaths on 'chemical leaks' or other 'incidents' and 'medical accidents'. That kind of thing."

Darren scratched his head. "That's horrible and everything, but what's that got to do with me? I'm twelve. I wasn't even born then."

Marek smiled. "It has everything to do with you...and me. Tell me, where was your mother working when she was pregnant with you?"

"She was a dinner lady at this school near where she and Dad used to live. Yeah, then she became a nurse afterwards."

Marek grinned in a way Darren found unnerving. "No doubt she would have had school dinners there five days a week – meaning she ate the virus, the DNA adaptor, Darren. She ate the virus with the genes of one of Project Helix's chosen creatures in huge amounts, it seems. It didn't do anything to her because, being an adult, she had stopped growing long ago. Any changes to her DNA would have no effect because her body was already fully developed, but..." He held up a blue hair.

"That's my hair!"

"I know. I tested it. Fascinating. Stronger than steel, fireproof and immune to cold. Truly amazing. Then I tested your DNA, Darren. There's a reason why you are so strong, why you can roar, why you prefer the dark and why you like to sleep under the bed."

Darren's skin went cold. "Stop! I don't want to know."

Marek tipped his head. "Are you sure? Even if it could explain how you were able to destroy a school with your bare hands?"

Darren hesitated.

Marek smiled. "I'll take that as a yes. Darren, the Project Helix virus your mother ate changed your genetic make-up. According to your DNA, you are twenty-one per cent monster!"

Darren's legs went weak. "Don't be stupid."

"Stupid? I'm far from stupid," Marek answered. "Come on, Darren, you must feel it. That you are different. That you have instincts others don't have. I tested your DNA – I'm telling you a scientific fact."

Darren shook his head. "But that would mean I really *am* a freak!"

Marek smiled. "I'd prefer you didn't use that particular word. That word is for fools who don't understand the power of being different. Who don't realize that if all people were as similar as they'd like them to be, the human race would have died out just like the dodo." He smiled. "What you are is unique, with twenty-one per cent of your DNA from some amazing, extinct animal that Project Helix seems to have kept secret from modern science... But you're not alone. My mother was, apparently, a primary school teacher in a small town near Krakow in Poland. Two years before your mother was exposed to the virus, *my* mother consumed some of the Project Helix virus containing alien genetic material."

Darren looked at Marek, wide-eyed. "You mean...?"

Marek nodded. "I am nineteen per cent alien. I'm unique too, but guess what – I love it! I can see ultraviolet light and I have an IQ of two hundred and ninety-nine. That's more intelligent than is humanly possible!"

Darren eyed Marek doubtfully. "Like...nineteen per cent some green, gooey, one-eyed blobby thing?"

Marek raised an eyebrow. "Well, I'm not sure about that. There are billions of planets out there, orbiting countless stars. No doubt there are many trillions of alien organisms. Some may indeed be...'blobby', as you suggest. All I can tell you is that Project Helix found one of the few aliens – perhaps the *only* one – ever to have travelled to Earth. Possibly the one that is rumoured to have crashed its ship in a place called Roswell in 1947. Whatever alien it was, it supplied nineteen per cent of my genes. Just as one of the various monstrous creatures who walked the Earth in ancient times supplied twenty-one per cent of your DNA."

"So aliens really have come to Earth?" Darren asked. He remembered all the alien invasion films he'd seen over the years. It felt strange, even unnerving, to find out some of it was true. "That's cool and everything…I guess…and it's fine for you if you like being different, but I'm not bright like you."

Marek grimaced. "Who told you that? Your teachers?"

Darren shrugged.

Marek waved a dismissive hand. "They're wrong. You just don't think the way they do. You don't think about what they think about. You don't even think when they think. You're not stupid, just wired differently. You have an extraordinary, monstrous intelligence that they'll never understand…and I need your help!"

Darren shifted uneasily. "I don't know about that."

Marek shook his head. "Darren, listen to me. This is important. Someone or something is trying to get rid of the last evidence that Project Helix ever happened."

"What evidence?" Darren asked, then his brain caught up. "Us?"

Marek nodded gravely. "We're the only remaining proof of what they did – they have to dispose of us. But if we work together, we can stop them from hurting us or doing anything like this again. Who knows what secret projects they are running now? You and I could be a formidable team – me with my vast intelligence and you with your monstrous abilities. Stop hiding under the bed, Darren, and come with me!"

Darren looked at Marek hesitantly. "Stopping them is really up to you and me?"

"Yes. Us, and only us." Marek produced a torch from his pocket and shone it at the wall. In the circle of light, the wall shimmered and became a swirl of constantly changing colours.

"What's that?"

"A little something I invented. It's a Sub Quantum Ultraionic Interdimensional Device…or SQUID for short. It can make two places millions of miles apart exist at the same point in space. You can then travel between them. Space travel, essentially."

Darren's jaw dropped. "That goes to another planet?"

"Well, no. I'd need to harness the power of a small star to do that. Since I'm running this off my phone battery, outside the prison walls will have to do. Come on, we need to hurry."

Darren looked at the swirling light and then at the bed. Under the bed was dark and safe. Not like the unknown beyond the light. *But it's only safe until they drag you out,* a voice inside his head reminded him. *You can't hide for ever.*

He stepped towards the light. "Is this safe?"

Marek considered the question for longer than Darren would have liked. "Well, it's always been safe for me, but I am part pandimensional being. The ultraionic beam is extremely powerful. However, with your monstrous skeleton, I'm fairly sure you'll be fine."

The circle of light continued to swirl. Darren needed time and somewhere dark to think. Aliens being real; secret organizations… It all seemed so big, so important, so unlikely – and it was all happening too quickly.

Marek whispered in his ear, "My phone battery is almost flat. Time's up."

A two-thumbed hand pressed against Darren's back. He tipped forward and fell into the unknown.

CHAPTER 4

PLAN B

Darren's face connected with something hard and cold. He rolled over, groaning, and sat up. For a moment he wondered if Marek had tricked him into headbutting his cell wall, but then he opened his eyes to find himself lying on a road.

The outer wall of Bleakmoor Prison rose above him. A circle of swirling colours was the only source of light. The heel of a polished shoe appeared in the middle of the circle, then a neatly ironed trouser leg followed and, finally, the rest of Marek.

The circle seemed to turn inside out as Marek withdrew his hand holding the SQUID and stepped over Darren. The light flickered and went out, plunging them into darkness. Darren stood up and looked around, his eyes adjusting quickly. The road stretched off to left and right, hugging the prison wall. Away from the wall stood a shed, and beyond that was the wide expanse of the moor.

"Right, yes, right... Hmmm. Okay, right. No need to panic."

Darren stared at Marek, who was rubbing his forehead with one hand. "Panic?" he asked.

Marek appeared startled and looked around. His eyes passed over Darren, but he didn't seem to see him in the darkness. "No, don't panic. It's all fine!"

"Er...you don't look fine."

Marek waved a hand. "I'm just trying to work out what to do."

Darren's jaw dropped. "You don't know what to do?"

"Well, no. I was intending to use the SQUID to transport us to safety. It has a much longer range if you don't have to go through solid objects, but you dithered and I ran out of charge. It didn't help how thick the walls were at Bleakmoor Prison. It took far more energy to get in and out than I expected."

"But you have a Plan B, right?"

Marek winced in Darren's general direction. "Well, no. My Plan A's usually work."

"NO?" Darren shouted.

Marek flinched. "Please don't shout. That was painful even to *my* ears." He looked thoughtful. "Maybe I should have charged my phone before I broke in…"

Darren approached Marek and bellowed, "We're miles from anywhere and you didn't charge your phone? You've just tripled how much trouble I'm in!"

Marek covered his ears. "Ouch? You panicking really doesn't help me think."

"You know what would help? A PLAN B!"

"Darren, listen. I have some excellent breathing exercises that'll help you calm down."

"Shhh!"

"No, really. Breathe in for eight seconds and breathe out for ten. It really works."

"Shhh!"

"No, honestly. Controlled breathing is—"

Darren covered Marek's mouth. "Someone's coming!"

Marek answered in a muffled whisper, "Where from?"

Darren pointed left and listened. "Two people. A man and a woman, I think. We need to hide."

"Where?"

"There."

"Darren, I can't see anything."

"What, nothing?"

"Nothing."

Darren took his hand. "Come on." He led Marek to the shed. It was empty. "Nowhere to hide in there." Darren looked at his bright orange tracksuit. It was sure to show up in torchlight. He lay down and rolled on the ground.

"What are you doing?" Marek asked.

"Rolling in mud."

"Seriously? Is this the time for pig impressions? Wait, I see them!" Marek pointed to a torch shining in the distance.

"I was right. A man and a woman," Darren whispered. He looked around the back of the shed. There was one wheelie bin. "Too narrow for me. You'll fit."

"Fit where?"

Darren opened the bin. "Here." He picked up Marek, who was remarkably light for his height, and dumped him in.

"Oh, this smells gross!"

"Stay silent, okay?" Darren whispered.

"Okay."

Darren closed the lid before Marek could say anything more. He looked around for another hiding place, but there was just the grass of the open moor. Two torches were now bobbing towards them. Two people meant he couldn't just keep moving around the shed to stay out of sight, as they might come at him from different directions. He looked back towards the prison walls and then ran silently over to them. The black stonework was old, worn by two hundred years of wind and rain. Close by, one patch of wall had worn away more than the area around it. It wasn't deep enough to be a hollow – more a curve in the line of the stone. With no better options, Darren pressed his back against it as the torches approached.

The man and woman moved close enough for Darren to hear their breathing as well as their footsteps. Darren closed his eyes and listened. He let his thoughts drift with the flow of the wind and the movements of small animals in the grass – a rat chewing on a bone and mice skittering this way and that. He began to breathe to the rhythm of his surroundings, bending his body, obeying the stormy swirls of air just as the grass did. He wasn't hiding. He was melting into the walls, the ground and air, until he wasn't there at all.

"Where did you say it was, Mr Ducas?"

"Another twenty metres or so, Miss Inghart," answered a man with a Welsh accent.

The man and woman emerged from the darkness. The man – Mr Ducas, Darren assumed – blocked his view of the woman, so that all he could tell was that she was tall, pale and blonde. He was average height, tanned to the point of being almost weather-beaten and was carrying a rifle with a torch attached to the barrel. He shone it along the path, the edge of its beam passing within centimetres of Darren's hiding place.

"Here?" Miss Inghart asked as they came to a stop less than a metre away from him. Darren's heart hammered as he recognized her. His mind tumbled. She had called herself Dr Wiseman, but now she was apparently someone else. Her accent was different too – she sounded Swedish. With a sinking feeling in his stomach, he realized that the only person who'd been at all nice to him since he'd demolished the school had lied to him.

"You hear that?" Ducas said, cocking his head to listen more intently. He swept his torch beam out over the moor. He passed over the shed and then swept back to it.

"You heard something over there?"

"No. I thought it was closer. The wind, maybe."

Darren focused his mind on the wind and the grass, melting again.

"I don't hear anything." Miss Inghart looked at the shed. "This is where the tracker said he was?"

"Yes, but it was almost out of his bloodstream. It was fading even when he was still in his cell. It only showed up for a few seconds out here."

Miss Inghart looked up. "This is right below his cell window?"

"Pretty much," Ducas answered.

"He could still be in there. He could be hiding. We know he does that from what he told me and his school reports.

The tracker software could have malfunctioned."

Ducas shook his head. "So the hidden camera in his room goes off three minutes before his tracker malfunctions and then comes back on seconds after we lose the signal completely? Unlikely."

Miss Inghart pulled out her phone and dialled.

"The governor, please. This is Dr Wiseman... Yes, hello, Governor. We spoke earlier about Darren Devlin. Yes, he is highly dangerous, I know, but I'm concerned about his state of mind... Nevertheless, could you have a guard check on him, now? Thank you." She cut the call and waited.

Ducas pulled out a phone. "I've got our camera feed from his cell. The guard's going in now..." He looked at Miss Inghart and shook his head. Seconds later an alarm sounded inside the prison.

Miss Inghart said something in a language Darren didn't understand and curled her free hand into a tight fist. "This is bad. Really bad! He could be anywhere. Check the shed, just in case."

"Understood," Ducas answered. He moved noiselessly towards the shed, his rifle raised. It seemed clear he was some sort of a soldier, or had been. He sidled up to the door and shone his torch inside. "Empty."

He moved towards the wheelie bin.

"Come on," Miss Inghart called. "He wouldn't fit in there."

Ducas paused, cocking his head again, and then obeyed. He made his way back to Miss Inghart with his rifle pointing down. He stopped, half-facing Darren but not spotting him. "What now?"

"We circle the perimeter in different directions. Stay close to the walls. If he's skulking around, we'll see him."

"Okay," Ducas answered. He watched Miss Inghart run off and muttered, "I should've filled him full of elephant tranqs back at the police station."

Darren watched the man jog away with long easy strides until he was out of sight. He breathed out and stepped away from the wall, then ran over to the wheelie bin and opened the lid.

"Don't take me!" Marek whined.

"Shush!" Darren hissed. "They're still close."

"Oh, it's you. Help me out, would you? I'm really wedged in."

Darren grasped Marek under his arms, yanked him out and plonked him on the ground.

"That was close," Marek said, looking around despite not being able to see a thing.

Darren glanced in the direction Miss Inghart had run. "I've seen that woman before. She said her name was Wiseman but the man she was with just called her Inghart. She said she'd help me."

A knowing look spread over Marek's face at Miss Inghart's name. "She lied to you."

"They were tracking me."

"Probably a radioactive tracker slipped in your food. Gamma emitters don't stay in your system long."

"She was the only nice person I met since this all started, but she just told the governor I'm highly dangerous...and that guy with her had a gun!"

Marek nodded. "They were at the police station when you were taken. They intended to kidnap you. They might have found a use for you for a while, but then..."

"I can't believe it," Darren whispered, but deep down he already knew it was true. "What do I do now?"

Marek smiled sympathetically towards where he thought Darren was standing. "Well, you can't break back in. You have to come with me."

Darren looked at this strange part-alien boy and sighed. "Okay."

Marek grinned and clapped his hands. "Excellent! While I was in the bin I came up with the beginnings of a Plan B. The nearest village is Bleakdale. We should be able to walk it in a few hours. Where's the Pole Star?" He pointed at the sky. "There it is. So it's this way." He began walking towards the moor. After six steps in the dark, he slipped and fell. "Ouch..."

Darren groaned and pulled Marek upright. "Hop on."

"Hop on what?"

"Me." Darren moved Marek's hands to his shoulders.

"Oh, okay. Piggyback?"

"Hurry up."

Marek unsteadily pulled himself onto Darren's back. "I've never done this before," he said nervously.

"Hold on," Darren ordered and ran off across the moor.

CHAPTER 5

A PERFECTLY NORMAL BREAKFAST

The grass of the moor sped by in a blur as Darren moved through the dark. Marek's arms locked around his neck reminded Darren of days long past when he had given Daisy piggybacks in their back garden. She had called the way he ran "lolloping". It was a word she had learned from her favourite picture book about a bear, and it somehow seemed right for the way he used his arms to help propel and guide him while his feet pushed him forwards.

He had won a race by lolloping on his first day at school. The other kids had laughed and called him a gorilla. That night his dad had told him it was time to be like other boys. From that day on, Darren had run every race upright on his short legs. He always came last.

Darren felt a sad hole open in his chest as he thought of Daisy, but the sounds of the countryside and the cold air biting deep into his lungs unlocked a strange sense of joy inside him that overwhelmed the sadness. This night, so far from the orange street lights of Farlington, was darker than any he'd ever known and it seemed to welcome him like a long-lost son. The leaves rippled and the grass rustled like music, while the calls of badgers, foxes and owls weaved into a song. He grinned and ran faster – thirty minutes, forty, more – forgetting Marek was there until the first hint of dawn appeared on the horizon, at which point Marek suddenly gripped him tighter.

"What's up with you?" Darren asked.

"I can see now."

"So?"

"You're going really fast. It's scary."

"We'll never get there if we slow down," Darren answered as he adjusted his direction to aim for the lowest part of a particularly high hedge.

"Please, just a bit? Watch out, there's a hedge!"

"I know," Darren answered and jumped. The laces of his trainers brushed the hedge leaves as he sailed over, while Marek screamed.

"Oof!" Marek groaned as they landed. "I think that crushed my equipment!"

"Sorry," Darren answered and lolloped on until a road came into view. He slowed and straightened, allowing

Marek to sink to the ground.

"Thank you," Marek said as he stood up gingerly and stretched his long limbs. "That was extraordinary, you know that?"

Darren shrugged.

Marek looked at him. "You just ran for over an hour and you're not even out of breath!"

"I'm quick when I lollop," Darren stated matter-of-factly.

"I think I prefer cars though. No offence," Marek said. "Speaking of which, that road should take us to Bleakdale. Come on."

They walked the last mile to the village the totally human way, with Darren taking two steps for every one of Marek's long strides.

Marek ran out of breath after ten minutes. "I don't think my alien side is built for walking," he said between wheezes. He took a puff on an inhaler.

The village was hardly awake when they walked in. There were only dog walkers and one shopkeeper to be seen.

"Let's find breakfast." Marek led the way, carefully avoiding a mongrel dog running in their direction.

The dog bounded up to Darren and stretched out its front legs, wagging its tail in the air. He'd never owned a dog, but he knew it wanted to play, so Darren rumbled in his chest, dropped onto all fours and pretended to bite the dog's neck.

It growled playfully and nipped at the collar of his tracksuit. He pushed it backwards and rumbled again. The dog rolled over, showing that Darren had won. He rubbed its chest and it panted happily before bounding away to its owner, who gave Darren a quizzical look as he passed. Darren got up off his hands and knees as casually as he could.

Marek was standing at the end of the road with hands on hips. He pointed to a pub on the corner.

"Looks closed," Darren said as he approached. "And we're not old enough."

"Don't worry about that." Marek walked to the door and knocked. He knocked repeatedly for five minutes until the door opened.

The owner stood there in her pyjamas, her face red with rage. "Do you know what time it is!"

"Six in the morning," Marek answered calmly.

"We don't open until eleven," she replied angrily. "And we don't let kids in unless they're with an adult!"

Marek tipped his head from side to side. His voice sounded different when he spoke again, as though it was coming from the air around him. "You are opening early today and we're older than we look."

The woman blinked. "You're in luck. We're opening early today," she said pleasantly and opened the door wide.

"Thank you," Marek said and entered.

Darren followed and watched, perplexed, as the woman happily set one table in the otherwise deserted restaurant and brought over two menus.

"I'll give you a few minutes to choose," she said and left the room.

"Was that a hypno-doodah?" Darren whispered.

"Hmmm? A hypnofield? Yes. Quite easy on one person." Marek's lips thinned. "I hate doing it."

"Why? It's cool."

"I've been doing it for years. It feels a bit unimaginative just going –" he flexed two of his long fingers – "'These aren't the droids you're looking for' every time you need to escape." He leaned back and looked out of the window. "I'm better than that."

Darren watched him closely. He was pretty sure Marek was telling the truth, but it didn't feel like the whole truth. He decided to leave it.

Marek plugged his phone in to charge under the table and then turned his attention to the menu. "What do you fancy? They only have lunch and dinner options."

Darren looked at the menu. To him it seemed nothing more than a swirl of colour with strange black squiggles all over it. He felt himself blush and hoped Marek wouldn't notice.

"I'm not hungry."

Marek frowned and looked up. "You ran for miles."

"So?"

Marek studied him. "Logically, that much running would make you hungry. We may not eat for a while. You should eat."

Darren pushed the menu towards Marek. Since this place didn't usually serve breakfast, he couldn't guess what might be available. "Choose me something, if it's important to you."

Marek's frown deepened. "Hmmm..." He pointed to a blackboard. "What about a meal from the specials board?"

Darren hardly glanced at the board. To him, the white writing was just gobbledygook. He blushed harder. "Nothing looks good."

Marek shrugged. "I can get her to make anything. What would you normally go for?"

"Dunno."

"Hmm..." Marek studied the menu. He clicked his long fingers to call the owner over.

"What can I get you, boys?"

Marek smiled slightly. "Beef steak for my friend here, please."

The owner sounded surprised. "Steak for breakfast?"

Marek's voice changed again. "It's perfectly normal to have steak for breakfast."

She blinked. "Steak? Good choice. How do you want it cooked?"

"Blue," Marek answered.

"Okay. How about you?"

"Eight pints of water, four straws, three spoons and an extra napkin, please."

"Eight?"

"Ordering eight pints of water for breakfast is also perfectly normal."

She blinked again and shook her head as if to clear it. "Well, that's all fine."

Darren watched her leave and then stared at Marek. "Um…"

"You have two questions," Marek suggested.

"Yeah… What does cooking a steak 'blue' mean?"

"They hardly put it in the pan to cook it. The middle will be raw."

Darren pulled a face. "Raw?"

Marek held up a menu. "You told me to choose."

Darren felt his face go hot. "Yeah, well…"

"Your other question?"

"Eight pints of water and no food?" Darren asked.

Marek leaned back and sighed. "Sadly, yes. All will become clear."

Presently, the owner brought the water. Marek watched

her retreat to the kitchen and passed one glass to Darren. "You must be thirsty."

Darren sipped his water and realized just how thirsty he was. He gulped down the whole pint. Marek passed him a second glass before picking up a straw and sipping from one of the six glasses remaining in front of him. He took another and poured it over his shoes. "That bin was horrid," Marek explained calmly, "and it's amazing how muddy you can get being carried across a moor. I just can't stand it." He took a napkin and wiped mud from his shoes.

Darren looked at the four untouched pints and wondered what they were for. Marek showed no sign of touching them, but instead continued cleaning his shoes.

Darren's curiosity got the better of him. "What about those four?"

Marek glanced at the pints. "It'd be impolite of me to eat before your steak arrives."

Darren fiddled with his napkin and looked at his own muddy tracksuit and trainers. He took a gulp of his water and decided he didn't have a hope of understanding the boy sitting opposite him.

Marek sat up and sighed. "That'll have to do. Ah! Here's your steak!"

When the owner had left them, Darren prodded the steak with a fork and looked at Marek. "Raw in the middle?"

Marek smiled and nodded. He took a packet the size of a small envelope out of his suit-jacket pocket, tore off the top and then poured the contents into one of the glasses. The brown powder floated on top of the water until he stirred it in. He then produced a second packet and poured its contents into a different glass. The white powder sank sluggishly to the bottom while Marek unwrapped fifteen sugar lumps and dropped them in one at a time. The moment the first touched the white powder, the whole glassful began to fizz and boil. Marek seemed unconcerned by this as he produced two more packets. One contained a blue powder, which he poured into a glass before adding table salt. This also fizzed and created an eggy smell. The final powder was made of very fine crystals. When Marek added it to the remaining glass of water, the resulting mixture turned solid.

Marek picked up a spoon and stirred each of the pints, except the solid one, which he hit hard with the spoon. The mixture disintegrated, glass and all, creating a pile of small shards. Marek used the spoon to shovel the fragments into the three remaining pints.

He looked at Darren. "Eat up. This will take a few minutes."

Darren decided not to comment and instead prodded his steak again before stabbing it with his fork and slicing off as small a piece as he could. The middle was indeed raw.

He closed his eyes in trepidation, never having eaten raw meat before, and placed the slice in his mouth.

The effect was immediate. His mouth watered and he suddenly felt entirely awake and full of energy. He opened his eyes as he gulped. The room seemed much more vivid to him than before. He heard a skittering sound and realized he was hearing a mouse running under a floorboard. On the far corner of the ceiling, he saw a tiny spider spinning its web. He looked down at the steak and growled before stuffing the entire piece into his mouth and swallowing. As the meat reached his stomach, he felt as though every fibre of his body was singing with joy.

"More!"

Marek grinned and clicked his fingers. "Another steak for my friend here," he said to the approaching owner.

Darren rumbled in his chest.

Marek raised an eyebrow. "Better make that five steaks."

"Blue again?" the owner asked.

"Raw, I think. In one big bowl."

Her jaw dropped. "Raw?"

"It is perfectly normal to order raw steaks for breakfast."

She blinked. "You want orange juice or tea with that?"

"We're good," Marek answered.

As Darren waited impatiently for the steaks, the lights in the room flickered and dimmed.

Marek tutted. "I thought so."

"What?"

"My phone's battery uses a lithium particulate super-matrix I invented. It's a little bit unstable, but it packs ten thousand times more charge than the standard version."

"Unstable how?"

"It can explode, but don't worry, I coded a safety program on my phone. The problem is that the electrics in here can't cope with charging it. I'm hoping we get ten per cent charge before the whole village's lights go out."

"Will that get us where we need to go? Er…where are we going?"

"London. I've set up a base there. It's entirely safe, but you need the SQUID to get into it. Ten per cent charge won't get us inside."

"Isn't there another way in?"

Marek shook his head. "No."

Darren rolled his eyes. "You know what another way in would be, right?"

"A security risk?"

"Plan B."

Marek raised his palms. "Okay, so I've learned something today. Plan B's are important."

"Yeah." Darren gave him a thumbs up and then watched his steaks arrive.

He'd speared the first one before the bowl even landed on the table and wolfed it down. His body sang again and the world seemed loud and vivid as he ate steak after steak. By the fifth, he wasn't even using his fork. He simply lifted the steak with his teeth, shook it fiercely from side to side and growled a laugh before flicking it into the air and swallowing it whole. He slumped in his chair, feeling more full than he could ever remember.

"That was awesome!"

Marek smiled a little sadly. "I'm not saying a salad would do you any harm, but you are mainly a carnivore. You're lucky. Both your monstrous and human heritage are mammal, so I'm guessing your digestive system works fine." He dipped a spoon into the brown pint, which had turned solid along with all the others. He lifted a jelly-like spoonful and ate it. The look on his face told Darren it didn't taste good. "*My* human and alien digestive systems don't work well together. I can't eat normal food. It causes havoc with my insides."

"Oh," Darren answered, not knowing what else to say.

Marek took another mouthful. "*Oh* indeed. I'm intolerant to lactose, gluten and eggs. Seeds and nuts bring me out in a rash and just don't let me near a strawberry. You don't want to see the results."

"Okay," Darren replied, wondering how near a strawberry Marek had to be for it to be a bad idea.

"My lungs aren't much better. My hay fever is a nightmare. Speaking of which –" he pulled a syringe out of a pocket – "this is full of xenodrenaline."

"Zeno what?"

"Xenodrenaline. If I have a severe allergic reaction, inject this into me and I should recover."

"Inject you where?"

"One of my buttocks," Marek stated calmly. "Anywhere else leaves a terrible bruise."

Darren pulled a face. "Please stay away from strawberries."

"I'll do my best." Marek put the syringe away.

Darren watched as Marek ate spoonful after spoonful from different glasses. "What's that stuff, then?"

"Oh, just a mixture of nutrients. Proteins and complex carbohydrates for my human digestion. Various metals and some silicon for my alien side. A lot of other things. I can only guess that my alien forebears came from a planet rich in them all."

"It doesn't taste nice, does it?"

"No." Marek pulled a face. "Maybe I should try adding pepper."

He was almost finished when the pub lights flickered and went out.

"Ah," Marek said and retrieved his phone. "Nine per cent charge before it melted the wiring." He looked out of the window. "Yes, looks like the whole village is down. We'd better get out of here."

The owner brought them the bill. "Cash, I assume, lads?"

Marek's voice changed as he answered. "You offered us a free meal."

She blinked. "Like I said earlier, this one's free. I hope to see you soon."

Darren followed Marek out to the road. "You need to pay her."

Marek stopped waving his phone around, looking for a signal. "Why?"

"We ate her stuff. Woke her up as well…"

"We're on the run and trying to save the world from a malign secret organization. Our need is greater. Come on. I can't get a signal."

Darren stopped dead. Marek walked on for a while before noticing his companion wasn't following.

"What now?"

"We need to pay her. We ate her food and trashed her electricity."

"None of that's important. We don't have time for this!"

They stood staring at each other until Darren tried a different way to explain. "We're trying to hide from that man and woman, right?"

"I suppose you could say that, yes."

"So why have anyone else complaining about us? Plus it's the right thing to do."

Marek thought for a moment and sighed. "Very well… I'll hack into her bank account and transfer a thousand pounds."

"You've got a thousand pounds?"

"I have an awful lot more than that."

"What?"

Marek waved a dismissive hand. "I am a genius, remember? I make money on internet trading."

"Trading what?" Darren asked.

Marek shifted uncomfortably. "If you're worried about me not paying a restaurant bill, I think it's best you don't ask."

Darren frowned. "You mean—"

Marek interrupted. "We'd better get going. We don't know if we're being followed." He pointed. "Take me that way."

"Take you?"

"Yes – you know, piggyback me," Marek clarified.

Darren shook his head. "We walk."

Marek raised an eyebrow. "That'll be slower."

"I don't take orders and I'm not a horse."

"Oh," Marek answered, looking genuinely surprised. Then his expression changed as he stared past Darren. "Umm…"

"What?"

"About hypnofields…"

"What about them?"

"They don't have a great range…"

"So?"

"…and they wear off."

Darren turned to see the pub owner storming down the road towards them. "Hey, you two! Stop, thieves!"

Across the road, a group of people waiting for a bus all looked up.

"I can't hypnotize them all without preparation," Marek added.

Darren ran his hand over his face. "So this is me saving you now, is it?" he said pointedly.

Marek looked embarrassed. "It looks that way."

Darren sighed. "Hop on!"

CHAPTER 6

THERE WAS NO MACHINE GUN

Miss Inghart watched from the BMW as Ducas swept across the field in a wide arc. She wiped mist from the window to get a better view as he crouched and looked at the ground and then jogged to the hedge.

He inspected the lowest part, finding something interesting in a few broken twigs, and then walked to a nearby tree. He climbed it rapidly and swung across a few branches before dropping out of sight on the far side.

Miss Inghart started the engine and drove a few metres to catch sight of him again. She saw him crouching, staring at the ground in the same way he had done every time they'd stopped to check that Darren Devlin's tracks were still leading to Bleakdale. She waited for him to jog back to the car and confirm they should drive on, but instead he signalled to her to come over. She got out, muttering to herself, and pulled her suit collar up against the wind. Unlike Ducas, she wasn't dressed for hiking; her well-polished shoes sank into the mud as she walked towards him.

"This had better be good!" she called.

He pointed to a patch of ground. "See here? The target finally stopped. He's got a weird running style, but I'm guessing he got here by maybe six o'clock this morning. Amazing stamina."

"You could've told me that at the car."

Ducas pointed. "See there?"

"I don't see anything."

"Yeah, the rain doesn't help, but that is definitely a footprint and it doesn't belong to the target."

"Are you sure?"

"Definitely. The target's feet are massive for a kid his age. Size fourteen and width J. That print there is size nine and width D. An adult-sized foot, but much narrower."

Miss Inghart looked at him as a strange feeling crept over her. "Long thin feet?"

Ducas looked up gravely. "Yeah. Are you thinking what I'm thinking, Miss Inghart?"

She nodded apprehensively. "I am, but we need more proof."

Ducas stood up. "They made for the road."

Miss Inghart took pictures of the prints. "Come on, then. Let's go."

Darren lolloped until the sun had nearly reached the height of midday. He came to a halt in the middle of yet another muddy field.

"Do these fields ever end?"

"Not far now," Marek replied as he dismounted. "Another hour, maybe."

"I need to rest."

"We don't have time," Marek said simply, without showing any sign that Darren's tiredness worried him.

Darren yawned. "I need to sleep."

"We definitely don't have time for that."

Darren ignored him and made his way to a hedge. "This'll do."

"You can't be serious?"

"Yup," Darren answered. He rolled into the dense hedge and pulled branches down around him. They seemed to hold him, keeping him safe.

"How long will you sleep for?" Marek called.

Darren closed his eyes. "I'll tell you when I wake up."

"Oh, I suppose I'll just stand here in the middle of the countryside and...and...well, keep watch," Marek snapped.

"Good idea," Darren muttered sleepily, melting into the world around him. Deep below him, he heard the gentle breathing of a family of badgers in their sett. In some distant place, he heard Marek continue to complain, but the sound of the badgers and the call of birds nesting around him carried him away into a deep sleep.

As Miss Inghart walked along Bleakdale's main street, a high-pitched whistle split the peace of the village – Ducas. He beckoned her towards a pub, where he was standing with a woman Miss Inghart assumed was the owner.

Ducas shook the woman's hand and walked towards Miss Inghart as she got close. "The target definitely isn't alone. That lady served them breakfast before they skipped town. Sounds like she was hypnotized. They made her open up early, ate a load of steak and now her electrics are blown. She thought they'd left without paying, but she's found a deposit of a thousand pounds in her account and a message saying *Thanks for breakfast*."

"She must be pretty confused."

Ducas nodded. "You can say that again."

"It's not our old friend's style to pay for breakfast. Did she ID them?"

"She did." He passed her his phone with two pictures on the screen.

Miss Inghart smiled with the satisfaction of having her suspicions confirmed, but her smile wasn't happy. She pulled out her own phone and made a call. "We have a positive ID. It's Marek Masters…" She listened for a few moments and then finished the call without speaking further. They walked in silence to the BMW.

"What are our orders?" Ducas asked as they reached the back of the car.

"We go after them both, but only Devlin needs to be brought in alive."

Ducas smiled grimly. "Good."

Miss Inghart didn't answer. Memories of Marek swirled in her mind. He would be fourteen years old now and she wondered how he might have changed since she'd last seen him. How much darker his soul might be after two years alone and on the run – if he had a soul at all. She had underestimated him back then, despite everything she had known. An uncomfortable feeling of anxiety gripped her. If Marek was pulling Darren Devlin's strings, she knew she must only be able to see part of the chessboard on which she and Marek were now playing. The order to kill him at least made things simpler. It meant Marek was Ducas's problem, and her partner was too direct to worry about Marek's mind games.

Ducas watched her with a thoughtful expression, and for a moment she wondered if she saw doubt or distrust in his eyes. Then he turned away, his thoughts his own, and opened the secret compartment in the car boot. He rapidly checked the firing mechanism of his dart rifle and lifted out two sets of darts. One, Miss Inghart recognized as elephant tranquillizers. The others were black and marked with a skull-and-crossbones.

"What's in the black darts?"

Ducas carefully lifted one for closer inspection. Up close, Miss Inghart could see that the logo on the dart wasn't a skull-and-crossbones. Instead, it was a bald, domed alien head with large oval eyes above the single letter X.

"Xenocide," Ducas answered. "I've killed Marek before. This time I want to make sure it's permanent."

Darren woke wondering if it was a school day. He hoped it was a weekend day, the kind where he got to stay safely hidden under his bed until lunchtime, when Daisy got back from her ballet class and Mum came home from her night shift at the hospital. A day without trying to read or write, when he could sit and listen to punk, or maybe muck about a bit with Daisy.

Slowly, memories of the last few days and hours

came back to him. He rolled out of his hiding place and yawned loudly enough to make birds fly away in a flurry of panic.

"There you are!" Marek picked his way through the mud towards him. "Four hours – really? We need to get going before they catch up."

"Give me a minute," Darren answered and stretched, allowing a low growl to escape him as his muscles loosened.

"Come on. I've been walking in circles for hours working out all the different ways the people chasing us might kill me while I don't have my tech working to fight back. At this rate, I'll die of a heart attack and save them the trouble!"

A question occurred to Darren as he watched Marek twitching with nervous energy. "Aren't you tired?"

"No. A bit achy from the piggybacking. That's all."

"Don't you sleep?"

"Not really. Maybe a couple of hours every few days. Seems like a terrible waste of time to me."

"Sleeping is my favourite bit of the day."

"That's lovely, Darren," Marek said waspishly. "This really is a lovely chat, but WE DON'T HAVE TIME!"

"All right."

"Great!" Marek walked behind Darren and got ready to jump on his back.

"I just need the loo first."

"Seriously?"

"Yup."

Marek placed his hands on his hips. "Can't you hold on for a few days?"

Darren raised an eyebrow. "Can you?"

"Yes. And I don't see a public toilet, do you?"

"I'll just use the hedge," Darren answered, feeling like he was stating the obvious.

Marek pulled a face. "Oh, that's disgusting!"

Darren shrugged. "Countryside rules," he muttered, and walked off. He could still sense Marek's disgust, so he jumped over the hedge and walked towards a large tree to relieve himself. As he wandered back, he watched the part-alien boy, in a suit and leather shoes. Marek seemed even more out of place in the country than he had in Darren's prison cell.

The sound of a distant car caught Darren's sensitive ears. Listening properly, he decided it was a van, and from the revving of the engine it was driving quickly along the narrow country lane that ran twenty metres behind him, only separated from him by an overgrown ditch.

As he ducked down to hide from the van, he heard a second, much quieter purr of an expensive car. The sound was moving slowly, as though the driver was letting the car coast along as quietly as possible. Darren grew nervous as he listened. It wasn't an ordinary sound – the car was *prowling*.

He turned to shout to Marek that they needed to hide, but the words died in his throat, because coming over the ridge, halfway across the field, was Mr Ducas, moving with slow, deliberate steps towards Marek. His rifle was raised, his head bent over the gunsight.

Marek, absorbed in his phone, was wandering aimlessly back and forth, entirely unaware of the threat. Ducas was easily close enough to fire, but fortunately for Marek a tree stood in between them. As Marek meandered about, Ducas was constantly having to adjust his aim.

Darren started to lollop towards the hedge, staying low to remain hidden from view. Ducas was now creeping away from the tree to get a better angle for his shot. He would be in position in seconds. Darren sped up, the ground blurring as he did so, and aimed for Marek, who continued to play with his phone, oblivious to everything.

Ducas steadied his gun and squeezed the trigger as Darren jumped, clearing the hedge and growling. As though in slow motion, he saw the black dart flying towards Marek. Marek looked up at the sound of Darren's growl and raised an arm to defend himself, just as Darren barrelled into him, knocking him flat. A sharp pain radiated through Darren's shoulder. For a moment, the gunman stood open-mouthed, but then he reloaded, this time with a green dart.

Darren picked Marek up by his belt and launched him over the hedge. "Run!" he shouted, and then lolloped away, keeping close to the hedge, dropping in and out of the ditch, hoping that he would now be Ducas's target. A dart thudding into a branch only centimetres above him told him he was. He zigzagged, instinctively knowing this made him harder to hit, and lolloped faster, before leaping back over the hedge. A dart brushed his cheek as he rolled in mid-air and landed at full pace. He looked across the field and saw Marek running like a badly-strung puppet towards a brightly-coloured van. It slowed as he waved it down.

Darren rushed in a zigzag towards the road, hoping the van would wait to pick him up too. He jumped the ditch onto the road and saw a BMW now parked on the verge. Miss Inghart was standing in front of it with something in her hand. It took him a moment to realize what it was, and in that moment Miss Inghart fired. A metal dart flew towards Marek as he opened the door to climb into the van, and suddenly split into a web of metal threads large enough to trap him.

Darren winced, waiting for Marek to be wrapped in metal wire, but it didn't happen. A circle of swirling colours appeared behind Marek and the web disappeared into it. Miss Inghart lowered her weapon, looking confused, and then ducked as a circle of swirling colours appeared beside her. The web exited the circle and now wrapped itself around her and the front of the BMW. Darren lolloped the final metres to the van as the driver began to pull away.

A crackling sound filled the air and bullets thudded into the driver's side of the van. Darren leaped for the back and his nails sunk into the metal roof. He moved along the top of the van towards the still-open door and let Marek pull him inside as they rounded a bend and drove out of sight.

Miss Inghart shuddered repeatedly as electric shocks pulsed through her. She heard footsteps approach.

"Hang on," she heard Ducas say. "Just trying to isolate the current."

The shocks stopped and she groaned as her body relaxed. She felt a hand gently grab her by the shoulder and roll her over, and she opened her eyes to see Ducas looking down at her.

He inspected the netting. "I'll get some cutters. You're all tangled up with the car."

The moment he'd cut away enough netting, Miss Inghart sat up. She closed her eyes as her head immediately spun.

"Take it slow," Ducas advised.

"Stop fussing! They got away clean?"

Ducas held up the sub-machine gun. "I hit the van, but didn't manage to disable it."

Miss Inghart narrowed her eyes. "You missed."

Ducas nodded towards the stunweb. "So did you."

"That's different. Marek used some kind of device."

Ducas shrugged. "No change there, then. Monster boy has some interesting moves. He saved Marek's life."

"Really?"

"Yeah, and he tried to draw my fire."

Miss Inghart grimaced. "They're becoming a team."

"Yeah. Bad news."

"Very," Miss Inghart agreed.

Ducas looked towards the road. "There's three different ways they could have gone from here. Did you get the van's registration?"

"Of course I did."

Ducas retrieved her stun pistol. "So, what now? The stunweb will have shorted out our car's electrics, so it looks like we're on foot."

Miss Inghart pulled out her phone. "It's time we called in some favours."

Darren struggled to get himself the right way up and wedged himself in by Marek on the passenger seat. Over the roar of the engine, he heard the driver screaming as he drove on at breakneck speed.

Marek's voice changed. "There was no machine gun. There was no machine gun. There was no machine gun…"

As he repeated the words over and over, the driver's screaming got quieter and then abruptly stopped.

Marek continued in his hypnotic tone. "You'd like to help us get to the hospital."

The van driver blinked. "You lads need a lift to the hospital? It'd be no bother. It'll only add twenty miles to my journey."

"Very kind!" Marek answered with a smile.

Darren leaned across to whisper to Marek. "We can't stay with this guy for long."

"Why not?"

"Too dangerous. We can't get him involved."

Marek rolled his eyes. "I'd rather we get some distance between us and the machine gun before we worry too much about that."

Darren heard the man scream, "Machine gun? Aarghhhhhhhhhhh!"

Marek's voice changed. "There was no machine gun. There was no machine gun…"

A few moments later, the man was chatting as though nothing had happened.

"So why do you need a hospital?"

"He fell," Darren explained.

"I fell," Marek agreed.

"He hurt his finger."

"My finger? Oh, yes. My finger. It's really sore." Marek lifted one long, perfectly straight finger. "I think it's broken."

The man frowned. "Okay…"

They drove on in silence for a while until the man asked, "You okay with the radio?"

"Good idea," Marek agreed.

Once a song came on, Darren hissed, "Why a hospital?"

"I need an energy source. I'll explain when he can't hear us," Marek whispered, jabbing a thumb in the driver's direction.

"Can't you just hypno-thingy him so he doesn't ask us any questions or remember anything?"

Marek answered in an exasperated whisper that grew louder as he spoke. "What do you think I *am* doing? It's easy to hypnotize someone to do something similar to what they usually do, like serve you food at breakfast rather than lunch. It's a lot harder when it's *not* something they would usually do. This guy clearly doesn't normally pick up hitch-hikers and I've maxed out what his brain can cope with to suppress the memory of the machine gun!"

"What was that? Machine gun? Aarghhhhhhh!" The van began to swerve erratically.

"There was no machine gun. There was no machine gun...."

The man relaxed. "Been a busy day for me," he said conversationally. "I had a kid's party at ten o'clock. Had to get the bouncy castle down in time to set it up for a fun day tomorrow."

Darren looked behind him into the back of the van where the bouncy castle was stored. He suddenly felt guilty at the thought of the castle failing to inflate at a fun day because of bullet holes.

The driver glanced over at them. "You two having an interesting day then?"

Darren and Marek looked at each other for a moment and burst out laughing. Darren felt all the fear and strangeness of the day flood out of him, while beside him Marek slowly drifted from laughing to crying. They finally lapsed into silence. The man gave them a funny look and drove on. "Kids!" he muttered.

Marek's voice turned strange. "We are not discussing anything you want to listen to," he said to the driver and then he turned to Darren. "Er, Darren?"

"Yeah?" Darren whispered back.

"Thank you for saving my life."

Darren grinned. "No problem."

Marek's eyes narrowed. "What's that in your shoulder?"

"What?"

"Don't move," Marek ordered, and he reached behind Darren. "I'll just—"

Darren felt a sharp pain. "Ouch!"

Marek leaned forward and showed him a black dart that he was holding carefully between finger and thumbs. "I didn't realize he'd hit you," he said, and held the dart out over the dashboard. A single bead of liquid formed on the black plastic.

"What is it?" Darren asked, lowering his voice.

Marek peered closely at the liquid. "Poison," he said quietly.

"So why aren't I dead or paralysed or something?"

"Because, judging by the way this liquid is scattering the sun's ultraviolet light, this is *xenocide*."

Darren looked at him blankly.

"Poison for aliens. Harmless to humans and other mammals. Lethal to me," Marek explained, and then looked out through the windscreen thoughtfully. "They really do want me dead."

Darren wasn't sure what to say, so he kept quiet and listened to the music. It was the kind of radio station where a DJ talked about pointless stuff in between playing pop songs. He listened to track after track and longed for his room, where every day after school he would crawl under his bed and let his music wash away the humiliations of the day, until his mum called him down to dinner and he had to face the dreaded question from his dad: *"Darren, how was school?"*

Darren was pulled back to the present by a song stopping mid-verse.

The DJ's voice cut in. *"Er…okay…we've been asked to hand over to Donna in the Blast 102 newsroom for an urgent newsflash. Donna?"*

"Thanks, Reggie. We're interrupting this programme to bring you news of a breakout from Bleakmoor Prison. Darren Devlin, a juvenile offender who was awaiting trial for serious criminal offences, escaped in the early hours of this morning. Devlin, who is suspected of destroying a school in West Fenshire, is described as extremely dangerous and should not be approached. Police believe he is being aided by Marek Masters, also known by the aliases Master M and Marek the Magician. Masters is wanted in twenty-nine countries for computer hacking offences and fraud. He is also considered dangerous and should not be approached. They are believed to be heading for Holdsby…"

The van driver whistled. "We'll have to keep an eye out for them."

The newsreader continued: *"Devlin is described as being twelve years old, fairly short and very broad with blond hair that can appear blue in certain light. He is likely to be wearing an orange tracksuit. Masters is described as being fourteen years old, tall and thin. He is likely to be very well dressed. If you see them or have information on their whereabouts, text the following number…"*

Darren reached across and changed the channel. He whispered to Marek. "Hacking? In twenty-nine countries?"

Marek frowned and counted in his head. "Yes, that's right. I'd forgotten about Iceland."

Darren stared at him. "Why did you hack Iceland?"

"Because they're in NATO."

Darren looked at him blankly.

"NATO – you know? The military alliance between North America and Western Europe?"

"Don't tell me, there are twenty-nine countries in NATO?"

"Actually, there were thirty at the time, but the French haven't noticed I hacked them yet."

"NATO includes here and the USA?"

Marek nodded.

"What did you hack?"

"Their military computers…mostly…and various other government things. You know, the FBI, MI6 and so on," Marek answered as though it should be obvious. "Except Iceland. They don't have an army or spies, so I hacked the coastguard."

Behind him, Darren saw the driver steal a worried glance at them. "Er, Marek?"

Marek looked puzzled and then said, "Oh," and turned to the driver. His voice changed. "We aren't the boys they are looking for."

The driver blinked and lost interest in them. He drove on. "We'll be in Holdsby soon."

"Thanks," Marek said and turned back to Darren. "Don't worry about the hacking. I was looking for information. Some insurance."

Darren frowned. "Insurance?"

"Information governments wouldn't want people to know, that I can use against them. So they won't come after me."

Darren thought for a moment and then asked suspiciously, "What kind of information?"

Something in Marek's manner unnerved Darren as he smiled knowingly. "It's best you don't know."

Before Darren could answer, the driver began to whimper and then drove right through a red light without stopping as they entered Holdsby.

Marek slipped into his hypno-voice. "Pull over immediately," he commanded. He turned to Darren as the van slowed and pulled in. "He can't cope with such an intense hypnofield. If we carry on, his brain will overheat."

"We're walking then," Darren said and opened the door.

Marek followed Darren out onto the pavement. His voice changed again as he leaned back in to speak to the driver. "You are tired. You are going to have a nap before driving on... We are not the boys they are looking for... There was no machine gun."

He slammed the door and joined Darren. "Hopefully he'll sleep. If he doesn't, we've got five minutes until he starts screaming again. I suppose you want me to pay for his petrol?"

Darren nodded. "And the van."

"What, for a few bullet holes?"

"Yup... And the bouncy castle."

"I'm sure the bouncy castle will be insured."

Darren shook his head. "Not against bullet holes."

Marek sighed, looked at the name on the side of the van and tapped his phone. "Done. I've had to estimate the value of the bouncy castle, I'm afraid. Now let's get to the hospital."

Marek led the way, navigating with his phone. "This way. There's no CCTV on this street. We don't want to end up on camera. The police will be monitoring it."

"Are you going to explain, now?"

"What?"

"Why the hospital?" Darren asked as they walked.

"They have a heavy-duty power supply and anyone is

allowed in. It's my best bet to properly charge my phone. Even if we can't get to the mains hub, they'll have a backup generator in case of power cuts."

"They'll have CCTV too, won't they?"

Marek nodded. "Yes, but if we trip the fire alarm, we'll have the place to ourselves."

Darren stopped. "You're going to evacuate the hospital?"

"Yes."

"No!"

"What do you mean, 'no'?" Marek asked, turning towards Darren.

"You can't make them move the patients."

"Why not?" Marek asked in a mystified tone of voice.

"Because they're ill! You know how you feel when you're ill, right?"

Marek shook his head. "No, not really."

"You've never been ill?"

"No. I don't think viruses and bacteria like my part-alien biology. So I don't get ill."

Darren took a moment to process this new information. "Well," he tried to explain, "when you're ill, all you want to do is hide under your duvet, and that's if you've just got a cold. Some of those people will be really sick."

"I'm still not seeing the problem."

"If they have to be moved, some of them might *die*."

Marek pinched the bridge of his nose in frustration and then let his long arms flail as he shouted, "Honestly, Darren! How are we supposed to stay ahead of the two assassins tracking us and half the country's police force if we keep stopping to pay our bills and make sure nobody dies? Where are your priorities?"

Darren stared back, feeling his anger rise. A growl swelled in his chest. "Find another plan."

Marek took a step back, looking unnerved. Then his expression hardened. "As you've already pointed out today, I'm more of a one-excellent-plan kind of guy. If you want to do it a different way, you come up with a plan!"

They stood staring at each other. Neither moved or spoke. Then a council maintenance van drove past and parked outside a cafe, catching Darren's eye.

He looked back at Marek and matched his defiant stare. "I've got a plan."

CHAPTER 7

BLOWING BUBBLES

Marek inspected the high-vis safety jacket. "You've gone too far, Darren. I'm not wearing this."

"You have to," Darren answered as he and the three workmen Marek had hypnotized got out of the council van.

"There must be another way." Marek threw down the high-vis jacket and pointed to his clothes. "This is a Gieves and Hawkes suit from Savile Row – I rarely wear anything else. It is hand-crafted to fit my slender frame, individually tailored to my tastes."

"So?"

"Don't you understand the finer points of tailoring?"

Darren scooped up the high-vis jacket and shoved it into Marek's hands. "It'll cover up the mud."

Marek looked at his mud-caked suit, nodded to himself and pulled on the jacket. His arms extended out of the sleeves by fifteen centimetres, while his body looked like it had been wrapped in a brightly-coloured tent. "Not exactly tailored for the slighter-framed individual, is it?" He pointed to one sleeve. "What colour is this thing anyway? Radioactive vomit?"

Darren ignored him and walked away to help the workmen – Dave, Joe and Karel – put out orange safety cones.

Marek, still muttering to himself, climbed out of the council van and walked over to the hospital's backup generator. A few minutes later, it shuddered and then rumbled into life.

Once the cones were out, Darren joined Marek. Behind them, Joe, Dave and Karel started to dig up the concrete.

"Right, my phone's charging quite fast. That's good. The sooner I get out of this jacket, the better."

Darren looked around nervously. Now that they were following his idea, he felt oddly responsible for it working.

"How long will it take?" he asked.

Marek looked at the generator. "Depends how hot it gets. I'm pulling more energy out of it than it's built for." He pointed to a piece of rubber and wiring. "I removed the safety trip-switch or it would have cut out immediately."

"We're putting that back after," Darren said.

Marek rolled his eyes.

Darren glanced over at the workmen. Two were still digging, while the third – Karel – was redirecting hospital staff who'd come over to see what was going on.

"Just maintenance," Darren heard him saying to three nurses, who looked at each other and then went on their way. The sight of their uniforms reminded him of his mother. He pushed the thought down and turned back to Marek.

"How did you hypnotize them so well? We're not standing anywhere near them."

Marek kept looking at his phone and said to himself. "This is good. Twenty per cent charge already. Forty per cent would be great." He looked up at Darren. "What? Oh, the strength of the hypnofield? It's because they all believe it. I think it could be almost self-sustaining if you had enough people, but I've never done more than twelve at one time. Hang on…" Marek fiddled with the generator. It shuddered and groaned as he worked. "I'm trying to increase the current."

Over the din of the struggling generator, Darren's ears caught the sound of sirens. "Police. Come on!"

"Just seven per cent more."

"Quick!"

Marek looked up irritably. "We need the charge!"

Behind them, the generator groaned again, smothering

the sound of sirens. Darren watched as Karel shook his head and blinked. He tapped Joe on the shoulder.

"Hypno-thing is breaking down!"

The sirens were now growing rapidly louder. Darren guessed the police were only seconds away.

"Marek, no time!"

"Forty per cent. Great!" Marek detached his phone and let the generator slow to a shuddering halt. "I just need to plot coordinates to North London."

Darren dragged him away towards an alley as the hospital windows began to reflect flashing blue lights. The siren sounds were just around the corner. "Hurry!"

"I am! London has complicated architecture. If I get this wrong, I'll SQUID us into a brick wall."

Darren pulled him along and then came to a halt. The alley was a dead end. Hospital buildings rose several storeys high on three sides.

Marek pulled off his high-vis jacket and threw it aside. "Hide!"

"What about you?"

"Hide!" Marek shouted as he turned to face the sirens.

Darren pressed himself against the brick wall beside a cast-iron drainpipe. He cleared his mind and let himself melt into the background. The sirens reached an ear-splitting scream as two police cars entered the alley and screeched to a halt. A police van pulled up behind them, blocking any chance of escape. Armed policemen jumped out of all three vehicles.

Darren watched as Marek moved towards them in the centre of the alleyway.

The police were shouting now:

"FREEZE!"

"STAY STILL! STAY STILL!"

"HANDS UP!"

Marek stood with his hands in his pockets and watched them calmly, a smile playing on his lips.

"Hands up, kid! HANDS UP NOW!"

Marek slowly raised his arms. As his left hand eased out of his pocket, Darren saw some small black balls fall from the bottom of his left trouser leg. None of the police seemed to notice. They were too focused on the rest of Marek, and especially on his phone.

"DROP THE PHONE!"

"ON YOUR KNEES!"

Marek kneeled, still looking oddly calm, keeping his hands high above his head. His phone, in his right hand, glinted in the sun.

The police stopped shouting and waited, their guns aimed at Marek. Two people jumped out of the back of the van and Darren's heartbeat quickened as he recognized

Miss Inghart and Mr Ducas. Miss Inghart held back while Ducas ran forward with a dart rifle raised.

Marek laughed. "Why, Mr Ducas! So pleased to see you!"

"Don't you do anything stupid, Marek," Ducas warned as he approached. "Put the phone down."

Marek tipped his head to one side and slowly lowered his phone. He glanced past Ducas.

Darren followed his gaze and saw the black balls were now rolling between the police officers. As Darren watched, the balls began to float slowly upwards.

Marek fixed his stare on Ducas and leaned forward to place his phone on the ground. He opened his mouth to speak.

Ducas took a threatening step forwards. "No mind tricks, Masters!"

Marek's smile warped into a malevolent leer as he placed his phone on the floor and let his thumb gently swipe the screen. He pulled away and placed his hands behind his head.

From behind Ducas, there was a confused shout. The floating balls were now expanding rapidly. As they did so, they lost their colour, becoming see-through. One was expanding faster than the others. A policeman screamed as it touched him and sucked him inside. He began to struggle rapidly.

Another sphere touched a policewoman and she immediately froze. As the bubble engulfed her, she began to move in slow motion. Meanwhile the other trapped police officer was flailing around at terrific speed, as though on fast forward. Other bubbles were growing rapidly now, capturing police officers and even their cars, and the people and vehicles in each bubble were moving at different speeds. The fastest bubbles seemed to be darkening, as if daylight was already giving way to night inside them, while the slowest seemed almost frozen in time. Then the fastest-moving bubble touched the one holding the slow-motion policewoman and both imploded, sending out shock waves that sent cars and people flying.

Darren was pushed against the wall as a ripple from the blast hit him. He held onto the drainpipe as Marek, phone in hand, ran as fast as he could at the opposite wall. He didn't stop as he reached it, but instead pointed the SQUID and created a circle of swirling light to jump through. Darren could only watch as Ducas ran after him and leaped through the light as it began to fade, disappearing from sight.

In a gap between shock waves, Darren looked around at the scene of chaos. Marek's bubbles were still trapping police officers and cars before imploding as they touched. As he watched a van lifting into the air, Darren realized that he was no longer focusing his mind on hiding – and Miss

Inghart was sprinting right at him, weaving between the bubbles with snakelike grace.

With nowhere else to go, he climbed up the outside of the building, swinging from the drainpipe. He drove his short, hard nails into the brickwork and used his feet to push himself ever upwards. Miss Inghart skidded to a halt and aimed her stun pistol at him, but Darren sped up, pulling himself over the edge and onto the flat roof just as the crackling sound of the web hit the wall below him.

Darren caught his breath and looked around, wondering how best to escape. He could see nothing on the roof except one fat metal vent that rose two metres into the air. Suddenly he heard a grunt behind him. To his horror, he saw Miss Inghart hauling herself onto the roof.

He lolloped away towards the vent, hoping to escape down it, as Miss Inghart rolled upright and pulled out the stun pistol again. In the reflection of the vent, Darren saw something silver fly towards him. It split into six smaller darts, all connected by the spiderweb-like net of thin metal wire. Darren jumped and climbed the vent, his feet gripping either side to push him up. The darts hit the metal below him with six sharp taps, burying themselves in the surface. As the sixth hit, a surge of electricity shot from the middle of the web. Darren felt it pulse through his arms in waves and he lost his grip.

He hit the ground hard.

Miss Inghart was running towards him. Pain was rolling up into a ball of hot lava in the pit of his stomach. He felt it change from pain into something else – a strange superheated anger that pulsed through him. In his mind, the shadow of a memory surfaced – of him tearing down his school. He *roared*.

Miss Inghart fired again, but Darren was moving at blinding speed now, first zigzagging away from her, then towards her. Barely aware of what he was doing, he jumped and flung himself feet first towards her. He aimed for her chest, knowing instinctively that the force of his two-footed kick would send her flying across the roof. At the last moment she leaned back, her shoulders almost parallel to the ground, but she'd reacted a fraction too late – Darren's foot clipped her shoulder and knocked her flat. Yet even as she fell, she punched her right hand into Darren's side, sending him tumbling towards the edge of the roof. He rolled and pushed himself up, wobbling for a moment with one foot in the gutter, then toppled backwards off the roof.

The ground and sky blurred as he tumbled over and over. With every turn, the concrete came closer, until Darren knew he was a single turn away from hitting the ground head first.

CHAPTER 8

TRUST

Darren spun a final time and for a fleeting moment he was surrounded by swirling colours. He wondered if he was dead and then he emerged from the circle of coloured light and found himself not falling but skidding horizontally across a grey tiled floor. He slid to a halt, sat up and looked around. There was a small group of people in front of him, many of them open-mouthed in shock. Around them, other people hurried past seemingly oblivious to his unorthodox entrance.

A woman with a Scottish accent found her voice first. "Hey! What did you just…"

The group suddenly looked away and a few of them gasped as a circle of swirling light appeared on the brick wall in front of them.

"Ha!" Marek shouted as he emerged in a controlled skid

and shut down the SQUID. "Did you see that? I opened a portal for a moving target and still landed in St Pancras station!" He got up and dusted himself down. His large eyes fixed on the stunned onlookers. "Oh…"

Darren got up and shifted behind Marek. The group stared in renewed silence, but several were beginning to look nervous.

"Okay…what do we do?" Marek muttered out of the side of his mouth.

"Dunno."

A boy beside a worried-looking man tipped his head and frowned. "Which of you is supposed to be Doctor Who?"

Darren immediately pointed at Marek who rolled his eyes and answered, "It isn't 'Doctor Who'. It's just 'The Doctor'."

The boy gestured at the SQUID and tugged his father's hand. "Can I get one of those?"

Suddenly, Marek's eyes lit up and he made a dramatic flourish in Darren's direction. "Come on, pointless assistant, the TARDIS is this way!" He leaned towards Darren. "Let's go!" he whispered.

Darren followed him, glancing over his shoulder and waving at the crowd who erupted in spontaneous applause…except for an older couple who were trying to attract the attention of a police officer.

"We need to hurry!" he hissed.

Marek didn't answer, but seemed to get the message and increased his pace as he led the way out onto the street, where taxis lined up two-deep beside a queue of people. He pointed away from the direction most people were walking. "There's an alley up there, just past King's Cross station."

Darren ran to keep up with Marek as he strode off, not wanting to lollop in front of so many strangers. Questions tumbled through his mind about what had happened during their hospital escape.

Marek turned into the alley he'd pointed out and leaned against a wall to catch his breath. He took a puff on his inhaler and then pulled out his phone. "Right, I need a minute to line up the SQUID again."

Darren held his side as his ribs began to throb. "Miss Inghart almost got me. She's...I don't know."

"A lot tougher than she looks?" Marek suggested. "Mr Ducas is worse. Believe me, I know. Fortunately, I lost him inside the hospital."

"This is all too weird."

"Hmm..." Marek answered, clearly not listening. He was fiddling with his phone again. "I need to hurry with this. There's so much CCTV here that they'll have found out we're in this area by now. I just need to let this app run…" He suddenly looked up. "Hey, did you see my time bubbles?"

Darren nodded and glanced nervously at each end of the alley.

Marek grabbed his shoulder and gave a maniacal laugh. "Did you see? Amazing, weren't they?"

"What were they?"

"QUIET bombs," Marek explained. "Quantum Uncertainty Initiated Entropic Time bombs. Each bubble randomizes the passing of time. When they touch, they react against each other, because only one time can exist in a given space. So the difference in time is destroyed with a release of explosive energy." His eyes shone. "It's just fantastic how well they worked! I made them a year ago and I've been dying for a chance to use them. To be honest, using six of the eight I've made was a bit extravagant. I need some incredibly rare metals to make them, you see, but I got carried away!"

"Did you need to use them?" Darren asked.

"I don't understand."

"Couldn't you have just SQUIDed through a wall like you did afterwards?"

Marek sighed irritably and then counted on his fingers. "Firstly, I don't 'just' SQUID. It is difficult. Secondly, yes, I could have used the SQUID straight away, I suppose, but I wanted to see how the QUIET bombs worked." He grinned excitedly. "Wasn't it amazing? Generating pockets of time… I amaze myself sometimes! I think if I did that with smaller particles, I could probably make a tiny universe… That might even be how the Big Bang happened…but I don't have time to solve the mysteries of the universe. I've got things to do." His eyes narrowed. "Oh, and thirdly, I'll do what I like, thanks."

Darren rubbed his hand through his hair. "Yeah, but what about the police?"

"What about them?"

"You blew things up!"

Marek waved dismissively. "Oh, they were inside bubbles. Most of the energy explodes outwards after the initial implosion caused by the time-collapse. So they should be okay…probably…in a manner of speaking."

"That's just luck, though," Darren pointed out.

Marek pulled the SQUID from a pocket. He stood closer to Darren and stared at him with his strange oval-shaped eyes. "What's your point? Those people were pointing guns in my face, in case you've forgotten!"

Darren stared back at Marek. "You could have run away, but instead you did the bubble thing."

Marek tapped his phone and pointed the SQUID. A circle of swirling light appeared on the ground. He loomed above Darren as he said icily, "Maybe you're right, but think about it, Darren." He jabbed a finger at Darren's chest. "You could have run away from those school bullies, but instead you destroyed your entire school!"

"That's different! I wasn't myself when I did that."

Marek gave a cynical laugh. "Are you sure? Maybe that's the *only* time you have been yourself. We're not human, Darren. To them we're not quite human, so why should we obey their rules? Now, come on. We need to get to my hideout before my battery runs out again."

Darren stood rooted to the spot and watched Marek. The events of the single night and day they'd spent together swirled in his head. This boy had told him the truth about himself and given him his freedom, but this part-alien also hacked governments, hypnotized people and set off weird gadgets without seeming to care about what might happen. A feeling started growing deep in his stomach. A feeling he couldn't quite name.

"This hideout. You use the SQUID to get in?" Darren asked.

"Yes."

"And you use the SQUID to get out?"

"Yes."

"So how do I get out?"

"Obviously, I let you out," Marek snapped.

"You let me in and out? Like a dog?"

"I suppose so… What are you getting at, Darren?"

"Like a pet?" Darren asked.

Anger bubbled up in Marek's reply. "Darren, would you just stop thinking for yourself and jump in?" he shouted. "We don't have time for this! Please, just do what you're told!"

Suddenly the feeling in Darren's stomach had a name. Mistrust. He didn't really know Marek and he couldn't trust him. He looked past the other boy. "What's that?"

Marek turned and saw nothing, but when he looked back, he was alone. "Darren? DARREN! Darren, where *are* you?"

Darren watched, hidden behind a bin bag on the far side of the alley.

"DARREN! Come on! I know you're still here. We have to *go*!" Marek turned on the spot and then began to punch randomly at the air in frustration. The SQUID whined as he swung it around. Eventually, he calmed down enough to restart it and aimed it once more at the ground. "Last chance, Darren!" he called.

Darren remained hidden. He heard a car engine and footsteps running – someone had been alerted by Marek's shouts. A moment later Marek heard them too. "Your *real* last chance, Darren!" he shouted. "You must hear them!"

Then from the end of the alley a man shouted, "Hey, freeze!"

Marek immediately jumped into the light and a second later the swirling disc of colour was gone. Darren watched a bald man in a dark suit run to the spot Marek had used. He holstered a pistol and kicked the ground in frustration before pulling out a radio. "Control from Omega Team Leader. We lost them. Masters and Devlin are in the wind."

CHAPTER 9

THE LONDON NIGHT

Miss Inghart entered the headquarters of the Home Office and was handed a visitor's badge at reception.

"Good morning. Dr Wiseman, is it?" the receptionist said without waiting for her to speak. "For Department Ten?"

"It is," Miss Inghart answered with a smile.

"They'll be honoured," the receptionist said, smiling back. "They don't usually get visitors, but today they have two."

Miss Inghart smiled again. "I know my way."

She walked with her usual crisp efficiency towards the main lifts and then kept going beyond them until she reached what appeared to be a service door. She pushed through the door, then walked down two flights of stairs, which led to another lift. Its doors opened as she approached, then closed as she stepped inside, and the lift descended without her needing to press a button. The doors opened onto a small, brightly-lit lobby with three chairs lined against one wall opposite a single wooden door, which simply had the Roman numeral "X" written on it in gold lettering.

Standing at ease between the door and chairs was Ducas. He nodded slightly when he saw her. "Do all XSP field stations look like this?"

"Pretty much," Miss Inghart answered, and went to sit on an end chair. Ducas left her to her thoughts. She looked around the bare space. It was deliberately unremarkable, just like every part of XSP's web of influence, and all the other Department Tens based in companies and government buildings across the Western world. All of them hardly visited or talked about. All of them apparently without staff or a budget, but all of them there for an occasional visitor or two. Visitors who always seemed to know where they were going when they arrived, and didn't always leave.

Miss Inghart shifted nervously and, as if in response, the door swung open. Ducas glanced at her questioningly when nobody came out. She stood and led the way through. The room inside was as unremarkable as the lobby and even more sparse. The only furniture was a long table beneath a large plasma screen attached to the wall. The screen sprang into life as they entered. Miss Inghart waited with briefcase in hand while Ducas stood to attention, his back perfectly straight. He appeared to not even be breathing.

The image on the screen showed two women and a man on separate video feeds. There was nothing on their desks or behind them that would give any clue about where they were, except that the view behind the man showed the night sky of the southern hemisphere. Miss Inghart recognized her boss, Mrs Lahaine, and suppressed a shudder. As Head of XSP Covert Intelligence division, her reputation for ruthlessness was unrivalled and she did not look pleased. The two women were dressed in formal suits while the man, who Miss Inghart knew only as "the General", was in military fatigues. None of them spoke while the woman on the central video feed made notes on a pad. Unlike her colleagues to right and left, her face was blurred.

Eventually, the central member lowered her pen and spoke in an electronically disguised voice: "Begin."

The others leaned forward; Miss Inghart held her breath.

"Stand at ease, Mr Ducas," the General said quietly in lightly accented English.

Ducas immediately relaxed his pose. Miss Inghart chose not to move.

Mrs Lahaine spoke in the polished tone of a British aristocrat. "Miss Inghart, we've read your mission lead report and initial evaluation of Darren Devlin."

"Yes, ma'am."

"We've also read Mr Ducas's independent field operative report."

Miss Inghart glanced at Ducas. His face showed no expression.

"We have questions," Mrs Lahaine continued. "You had an opportunity to extract the boy in Farlington while he was in police custody."

"Yes."

"Mr Ducas advised that he could tranquillize the boy?"

"He did."

Mrs Lahaine removed her glasses. "You chose not to take the opportunity. Why not?"

Miss Inghart cleared her throat. "By waiting, I hoped to build his trust in me while he lost trust in his family and the authorities. It would have made him easier to work with."

The General cut in. "Working with him was not a mission aim, Miss Inghart."

"I realize that, sir."

"This was a Triple E operation. The aims were to remove him from society, study his physical characteristics, and then eliminate him. None of that required him to trust you. Now he's potentially been with Marek Masters for days!"

Miss Inghart's lips thinned. "It is easier to study someone's way of thinking if they are cooperative."

The General snorted. "Judging by his school reports, his ability to think is hardly important—"

"The boy does have skills…"

Miss Inghart looked in surprise at Ducas, who had interrupted.

"Sir," he added.

"Skills?" the General asked, clearly more interested in Ducas's opinion than Miss Inghart's.

"He was fast in open country and agile. Not just strong. He's good at hiding as well. Reminded me of how a fox can be right by you in an alley and you wouldn't know. He was standing five metres from me in an urban environment with little cover and I didn't spot him. That's as good as a top-class sniper."

The General considered this. "Is he tactical or is that all just instinct?"

Ducas shook his head. "I had limited time at close quarters. I don't know."

"Well," the General answered, looking again at Miss Inghart, "there's plenty we don't know…since he's still on the run."

Miss Inghart didn't answer.

Mrs Lahaine took over again, a slight tone of irritation at the General's interruption entering her voice. "Mr Ducas, before you lost sight of Marek Masters at the hospital, we note that you did not take a kill shot despite having a clear view of the target."

"Correct, ma'am."

"You chose not to take out Marek Masters, potentially the most dangerous opponent to our objectives in the Western world?"

"Yes, ma'am."

"Explain."

"We had tactical support from local armed police officers. They are not aware of XSP or its aims. I couldn't know how they'd react to me terminating a fourteen-year-old who appeared to be surrendering. The situation could have got out of control."

The central woman spoke. "I've heard enough."

Her fellow panel members immediately sat upright. Ducas stood to attention.

She continued. "Miss Inghart, you've been rebuilding your reputation since Operation Snowline. This is more than an unfortunate slip." Her tone hardened. "I am only keeping you in the field because you are an expert on Masters and he may still be aiding Devlin. Your priority is to bring in Devlin. We'll see if he can be trained, if he is as capable as Ducas believes. If not, he will be eliminated."

"Yes, ma'am. Thank you."

"Mr Ducas, to be clear, any opportunity to kill Masters must be taken. No collateral damage is too high."

Ducas didn't answer.

The central woman's tone hardened further. "Do I make myself clear?"

"Yes, ma'am."

The central woman sat back. "The clock is ticking. We are watching."

Most of the outside tables at the restaurant were occupied by couples. They chatted quietly as they ate, their words mixing into a general murmur. None of them noticed Darren as he padded closer, keeping to the shadowy doorways that stood just outside the range of the orange street lights. He watched them all eating, some couples laughing as if they had no cares in the world, while others spoke intently between awkward silences.

There was one family, sitting at a larger table. The father was reading a menu in irritable silence while the mother worked out orders for her son and daughter in between telling them off for being too loud.

"Will you be quiet, Harvey!" she snapped at the boy in a whisper that was easier to hear than anything the children had said.

"Mum, he's hungry, that's all!" the daughter replied, laying a protective hand on her younger brother's shoulder as his eyes filled with tears.

Darren's heart felt heavy. The sight stirred up memories of times Daisy had defended him. She always seemed to know what to say or do. Sometimes she had even stood in front of him while his dad was shouting and he would hide gratefully in her shadow, just like she'd always been there when the bullies had come hunting for him while teachers looked the other way.

He shivered at the memories and felt sadness well up inside him. He let out a long sigh and willed himself not to cry, but to be strong and stay hidden from the world instead.

A couple stood to leave, the woman pushing three purple-coloured notes under a vase. Darren advanced silently to the edge of the shadows. The only waiter walked inside, happy to leave clearing the table for a few minutes. Darren drifted up to the table, letting his breathing follow the rhythm of the general murmur of conversation. The couples kept talking, oblivious to his presence, while the family studied their menus. Darren reached out a hand and lifted a half-eaten burger from a plate.

"Hey, look at that boy!" The girl was pointing at him. Darren froze, burger in hand.

The mother looked up. "Oh my, George! It's that boy from the news!"

Driven by a jolt of panic, Darren ran into an alleyway, held the burger between his teeth and began to swing himself upwards, grabbing windowsills and drainpipes as he climbed. Above the level of the street lights, he was plunged into a protective cloak of darkness. He reached a roof ledge and sat to wolf down the burger. It was cold and overcooked, tasting of little more than charcoal, so he pulled out a half-empty bottle of water he'd found earlier on a park bench and washed away the taste. Far below, two waiters made a half-hearted attempt at searching the alley and then turned back towards the light and warmth of the restaurant.

From here, Darren watched the constantly moving river of headlights flow between buildings that rose like mountains towards the orange glow of the horizon. The view had a natural peacefulness that hid the reality of London below, with its noise, crowds and brightly-lit signs full of words Darren couldn't understand. Darren curled himself into a ball, drawing his feet up as far away from the London streets as he could, and let out another shuddering sigh. The sadness he'd felt while watching the bickering family surfaced again, like water drawn from a well. He clutched his massive hands to his sides and tried to summon a memory of his mum and Daisy holding him close in a group hug. The barest shadow of comfort the memory brought him finally helped him find the energy to stand.

He turned and looked at the far edge of the long roof. Beyond it stood the churchlike red-brick spires of St Pancras Hotel and the vast glass roof of the train station behind. He climbed down to earth, using a tourist coach as cover to drop the final few metres to the pavement. Then he joined the mass of travellers, letting the flow of the crowd draw him unnoticed into the train station, past expensive shops and coffee sellers. There, up high, were the departures screens. He knew the shapes on those screens spelled out the times and destinations of trains, but to him they were just a frustrating haze.

Somewhere, up there, he knew a departures screen said a train would be stopping at Farlington, but it made no difference. Even if he'd known which train it was, he couldn't read the platform numbers. Home, and Daisy, were out of reach. Frustrated with himself, Darren drifted out of the station towards the back alleys, which he was slowly coming to know. He stuck to the shadows as he walked along to the arch under a bridge near the train tracks that headed north, where his hoard of cardboard sat untouched. He burrowed into the middle of the cardboard and hugged himself once more, but this time the memories didn't help. The shadow of family comfort had already departed.

Miss Inghart sat at an empty table while Ducas studied the outside area of the deserted restaurant. She watched him work methodically from left to right and then linger in a doorway shrouded in darkness. She pulled her dark woollen coat around her to guard against the chill of the early autumn night and flexed her arm. It was still stiff and bruised from where Devlin's kick had hit her shoulder. She thought about him and the meeting at Department Ten earlier that day and let her mind flick through her options. Slowly, a plan formed.

Ducas strode over and sat opposite her. "He's been here before. The restaurant's a soft target for thieving if you hide in the doorways and escape down the alley. He hasn't moved far, has he? This is, what, eight minutes from King's Cross and St Pancras?"

"He won't come back now."

"No."

"But he's hiding around here somewhere. It's pretty impressive, don't you think?" Miss Inghart said. "It looks like he's doing this without Marek."

"Agreed. He wouldn't need to steal if Marek was with him."

"He's not been seen on CCTV once. Nobody evades us like this for over two days."

"So how do we flush him out?" Ducas asked.

Miss Inghart smiled humourlessly. "I'm thinking that we don't. We get him to come to us. First, I need to speak to his family, and I need you to monitor this area for signs of Marek."

Ducas frowned. "Okay. You're sure Marek's near too?"

"As sure as I can be. He'll look for Devlin." She paused and added, "Thanks for your support back at XSP."

Ducas studied her impassively. "I only bought you a few days. The General wasn't persuaded Devlin could be useful. Being Head of Tactical Operations, he values training and discipline. Trying to sweet-talk the boy was a bad call. Too risky, but I can see now why you thought he might be a valuable asset."

"It wouldn't have been risky if Marek hadn't turned up."

"He always turns up these days."

Miss Inghart looked out into the London night. "Seems that way. I need to use that to our advantage."

Ducas's face remained unreadable. "Can I ask you a question?"

"Depends."

"A hypothetical question."

"Okay."

"If you could bring Marek in and persuade him to work for us again, would you?"

Miss Inghart studied his eyes. They stared back at her, as expressionless as always. "Hypothetically, if I could change his mind, yes. Of course I would. He's an irreplaceable asset."

Ducas looked away thoughtfully and stood. "There's nothing hypothetical about my orders."

"I heard them too," she answered as he began walking away. "Mr Ducas," she called, but he kept walking. "Ifan!"

Ducas stopped at the sound of his first name, so rarely used. "Yes, Miss Inghart?" he said with calm coldness.

She placed one hand over her heart. "I haven't forgotten what Marek did."

Ducas stared at her for moment. "It would be difficult to forget," he answered. Then he walked into the shadows and disappeared into the night.

CHAPTER 10

COMING IN FROM
THE COLD

Darren huddled deeper into his cardboard burrow as the night brought its chill. Nearby, three railway workers in high-vis jackets started a small fire close to their Portakabin. The men, one tall, white and fair-haired and the other shorter and Black, laughed and joked, while their colleague, a pale red-headed woman, watched on with a stern but motherly air of disapproval, as though she was about to ban the fire at any moment. Over the last few days, some deep instinct had made Darren keep his distance from them, but now he longed to feel the heat as he watched them warming their hands. The need to be warm burned stronger than the suspicion he felt towards the three strangers, who talked quietly and occasionally laughed.

Darren carefully slid out of his burrow and crept to the edge of the light. The two men had pushed away all debris before lighting the fire, meaning there was no cover for him to hide behind. Darren took a deep breath and stepped forward.

"Hey, kid."

The taller man, on the far side of the fire, was watching him. He grinned, revealing two missing teeth. Darren watched him warily, ready to lollop away.

"You may as well come into the warm, kid," he said.

Darren hesitated.

The shorter man shrugged and pointed to a gap by the fire. Darren padded up quietly, keeping out of arm's reach, and let the heat warm him through his tracksuit.

The taller man smiled. "Is it you who's been sleeping under the arch?"

Darren nodded.

The shorter man whistled. "You're a quiet one. We were wondering who that was. You got a name?"

Darren hesitated, wondering if they ever got to see the news. The woman hadn't spoken yet and was watching him with a concerned expression.

"Man, you are rude," the taller man said to his friend. "I'm Grant."

"Robbie," the shorter man added.

Darren glanced warily at the woman. She smiled. "I'm Devina."

"Darren."

Grant grinned. "Darren? Okay. You don't get many Darrens these days. Good to have a Darren around the fire."

Darren let himself smile slightly and closed his eyes, concentrating on the warmth that slowly spread through his bones.

"How long you been out here, kid?" Grant asked.

"Two and a bit days."

"You been getting food?"

Darren shrugged again. "A bit."

"You need a coat," Devina said, moving closer. She eyed him thoughtfully. "You sure you want to be out here, Darren?"

"She's got a point, kid," Grant said. "There are shelters, you know, with kitchens and heating."

Darren shook his head.

Devina smiled. "How old are you?"

"Fourteen," Darren lied.

Devina glanced doubtfully at Robbie, who frowned.

"You avoiding trouble?" he asked.

Darren shrugged. "Sort of."

Devina looked sympathetic. "So, you need to get it over with. You don't want to be out here with something hanging over you. Sometimes a problem's not as bad as you think."

"This is."

Devina pursed her lips. "Robbie, Grant, can you help me with something?"

The two men glanced knowingly at each other and followed Devina away from the fire. Darren cleared his mind and let his sensitive ears tune in to their conversation while he stared into the flames.

"There's no way he's fourteen. I'd say twelve at most and he's a muddy mess," Devina whispered. "We need to get him to a shelter. It's not safe out here. Not for a boy his age. Either that or we need to call someone."

"I know," Robbie answered. "No, I really do. It's just you know what kids out here are like. If he gets even a hint we've called anyone, he'll run."

"True," Grant added. "It's not like it would be the first time that's happened."

Robbie sighed. "Maybe one of us lights a fire here every night till he trusts us?"

Grant scratched his ear. "I don't know. We're supposed to report people sleeping near the rail lines. Safety rules, you know? We could get sacked."

Robbie shook his head. "We could leave out some food and maybe a sleeping bag? You know, keep an eye on him? At least for a few days? I mean, if he's still here when our job finishes, *then* we make sure he goes to a shelter."

Devina sucked her teeth in disapproval. "Okay, but I'm

going to have a word with him!" She strode purposefully towards Darren while the others trudged after her.

"Listen, dear," she started, "if you let me help you find the right people to talk to, I'm sure we can work everything out. Believe me, a young boy like you? They'll want you back in. Back in school, back in care or whatever. You know what I mean? But you stay out here and a lot of really, really bad things can happen."

"Bad as they can be," Grant agreed. "Listen to Devina, kid. If you can, you need to get back in."

Darren watched the three of them and thought about how to explain how complicated his situation was.

"It's easier," Devina added. "A lot easier."

Darren sighed and finally a few words came. "I've never been in. Not really."

Robbie gave Grant and Devina a knowing glance. "All right. I guess we'll be here for a few days anyway – until we complete the signalling upgrade."

They lapsed into silence for a while until Devina checked her phone and then clapped her hands. "Last train of the day is coming through on the fast line, lads. We've got work to do!"

Robbie sighed. "See you, kid. Make sure the fire's out when you're done."

Darren watched the three head off for their shift and

stood alone at the fire, mulling over their words... *Bad things can happen...as bad as they can be.*

In the distance a dog howled. Then ten or twenty more joined in, each howl filled with a sense of distress that made Darren's skin crawl. In the next moment Darren understood the source of the dogs' pain, as a high-pitched ringing filled his ears. He growled and fell to his knees, the noise piercing his brain. Then the sound changed to a hollow echo and the pain subsided. And suddenly, as though it was wrapped in the middle of the hollow noise, Darren heard a familiar voice, speaking to him on a frequency that only his ears could detect:

"Darren? Darren, this is Miss Inghart. I need to speak to you. I need to explain. I need you to know that we understand. We all understand. None of this is your fault."

Darren lolloped away from the fire to his cardboard burrow and hid, but the words continued in his head.

"Darren, we know about Marek Masters. We know what he's like. Marek can convince people of anything. We understand that all those bad things you did were really Marek. Do you even realize that Marek met you before you destroyed your school? He hypnotized you, Darren. He made you do those terrible things."

Darren froze. Could that be true? Marek had said Darren couldn't be hypnotized, but could he have lied?

"*Darren? Darren, we know you ran away from him. We know you are beginning to realize what he really is and what he can really do. He is a psychopath and a manipulator, Darren. He manipulated you, just like he did that van driver – the one who really believes he saw a machine gun. There was no gun, Darren. You must know that now. People don't fire machine guns in English country lanes.*"

Darren frowned. He clearly remembered Mr Ducas firing a machine gun…or at least he thought he did. Could Marek really have planted the memories in his mind? Would he? But this was Miss Inghart. She had lied to him before, he knew that. He pulled the cardboard up over his head.

As though reading his mind, Miss Inghart's words continued:

"*I'm sorry, Darren. I'm sorry I said I was called Wiseman. Can I explain? I have been hunting Marek Masters for two years. He hates me. He has threatened my family. I have a younger sister I need to protect. My whole family now have to live under false names until Marek is caught.*"

Darren listened to her explanation and wondered if it could be true. He had watched Marek manipulate people. Now, as he lay alone in his cardboard burrow, he could imagine Marek being vengeful. He could imagine him hunting down a family. He could imagine him using a stupid misfit from Farlington to help him do it.

"*Darren, you have spent a day with Marek Masters. You know how little he cares about people and how he uses them. Don't let Marek be the reason you can never come home.*"

Home… The thought of it made his heart hurt. A question began to form in his mind. If Miss Inghart was really saying that everything had been Marek's doing all along, maybe he could go home?

"*Darren… Darren, please, come to St Pancras station. I am here. I am alone. I understand that you can't trust me yet. Trust is important to you. I know that, but I have a message from some people you can trust. Listen…*"

Darren listened, wondering, hoping.

"*Darren? It's Mum. We're so worried about you, darling! You need to come home now. Please trust the lady, Darren. We're trying to help you. We're all trying to help you!*"

Darren's burrow of cardboard exploded as he lolloped away as fast as he could.

Miss Inghart stood in the middle of St Pancras station and resisted the urge to scan the many entrances for Darren. Each way in to the station was being covered by teams of plain-clothes agents. She couldn't afford to give them away. She would have preferred a place with no crowds and a single entrance and exit, but she knew Darren wouldn't allow himself to be cornered so easily. She'd had to pick somewhere open and somewhere he already knew. St Pancras had been the only possible choice.

She opened the mic attached to her jacket collar. "Darren, I have a message from your father."

She played the message, converted into a high pitch meant only for Darren's ears.

"Darren, it's Dad here. Can you please come home, son? We miss you and we're sorry. We love you and I'm sure we can sort everything out. Just please, please come home."

In her earpiece, she heard her agents:

"This is Control. Teams, report. Do you see him?"

"That's a negative at Tube entrance."

"Negative on the walkway."

"Negative at taxi-rank entrance."

"Negative at main entrance."

"Negative on the bridge."

"Negative on the platforms."

"We see him! Walking alone. No, lost him. Where is he?"

"King's Cross entrance, confirm."

"He's in. He's definitely in. We lost him!"

"Concentrate, people!"

Then he was there, standing less than ten metres away from her. His orange tracksuit was horribly grubby and he seemed much wilder than he had been only days before. He stood still and silent amongst the passing commuters, who instinctively parted to avoid him. His expression seemed more bearlike than human, and for a moment Miss Inghart felt unnerved.

A voice crackled in her ear. Miss Inghart heard Ducas's distinctive accent. *"Target acquired. Clear shot. Sixty-three metres and a thirty degree down angle."*

"Hold the shot, Mr Ducas. Miss Inghart has the play. Code for shot is 'blue'. Let's bring him in voluntarily if we can."

"Copy that."

Miss Inghart crouched, lowering her eye level to match Darren's. He shifted his weight slightly, betraying something of his fine balance and animal power in the way he moved. Miss Inghart's pulse began to race as she estimated how quickly the boy could cover the distance between them. He cocked his head slightly, as though he could hear her heartbeat, and still he watched in silence.

Miss Inghart smiled and opened her palms in a gesture of friendliness. "Thank you for coming. Thank you for hearing what I have to say. Genuinely, Darren, I'm sorry. I'm here to take you somewhere safe. Somewhere warm. You must be so cold. I just want to work everything out. Please, come over to me."

Darren's expression became uncertain for a moment.

He suddenly seemed more like the boy she'd met in Farlington – young and scared.

"Darren. Come to me and together we'll stay safe from Marek. Once we know all about the time you spent together, you'll be able to see your parents. Would you like that?"

Darren nodded slowly and seemed about to move forward, but then his expression darkened and he rocked back a little until he was in perfect balance, ready to move in any direction.

"*Sniper, do you still have the shot?*"

"*Clear shot, confirmed.*"

"*Miss Inghart, say the word and he's down.*"

Miss Inghart gritted her teeth and got ready to play her last card. "Darren, I know it's hard, but please, even if you don't trust me, trust your sister."

She played her last message.

"*Hey, Darren. It's Daisy.*"

A river of emotions flowed across Darren's face. He took a step towards Miss Inghart's open arms.

"*I miss you,*" Daisy's voice continued. "*I want you to be able to come home and be safe and happy with me.*"

A smile flickered across Darren's face. He took another step as commuters passed between him and Miss Inghart, and Daisy's voice continued. "*About smashing up the school, you need to understand, they are telling us it's a Tiny problem.*"

Darren froze. His eyes scanned Miss Inghart's face. A commuter passed between them, and in the split second that her view was blocked, he disappeared.

"Blue!" Miss Inghart hissed into her mic.

"*No clear shot,*" Ducas answered. "*He's moving south. I've lost him. I can't see him.*"

"*Teams, report!*"

"*That's a negative at Tube entrance.*"

"*He's on the bridge! Repeat, on the bridge heading for the platforms.*"

"Take him!" Miss Inghart ordered, running towards an escalator. "Entrance teams, hold positions. DO NOT let him past you! Mr Ducas—"

"*Just behind you,*" Ducas answered.

She sprinted up the escalator, weaving past a man with heavy bags, and ran onto the bridge as Ducas caught up. He sprinted ahead of her across the bridge, his rifle hidden in a holdall. He came to a halt over three agents sprawled on the floor of the bridge. He kneeled for a closer look as Miss Inghart caught up.

"They're out cold," he said. "They didn't report getting into close quarters. He must've surprised them."

She looked around and spoke into her mic. "Does anyone have eyes on him?"

"*This is Control. That's a negative. He's gone!*"

She crouched and swore under her breath while Ducas swept the area. "Gone," he confirmed.

Miss Inghart stood up. "I almost had him! Something must have spooked him."

Ducas shook his head. "No. He read you. I saw it. He read the whole play."

"What? Are you a psychologist now, Mr Ducas?"

Ducas shrugged. "You need to accept it. You can't talk this kid in. He's too careful. We should have just dropped him with a tranq."

Miss Inghart didn't answer. Instead she rubbed her eyes.

"You know I'm right," Ducas pressed. "Even if I wasn't before, I am now. Every minute he's out there is a minute more for Marek to find him."

Miss Inghart came to a decision. "All right. He's a creature of habit, so he'll head back to where he's been hiding out. It took him six minutes to get here once I'd said I was at St Pancras. We know approximately how quickly he can run. So we draw a radius from here and flood the place with agents and police backup until we find where he's been hiding."

Ducas zipped up his holdall and patted her on the shoulder as he strode past. "Copy that."

*   *   *

High above the entrance hall, wedged between two metal struts of the glass station roof, Darren watched Miss Inghart and Ducas talking on the bridge. There was too much noise from train engines for him to hear what they were saying. Below them, he started to pick out groups of people, in threes, just like the men on the bridge, staying close to each entrance. A lot of them walked in the same military way as Ducas and they were all watching the crowds.

Darren prepared himself to spend hours hidden up high, just as he had done hundreds of times at school. He breathed out slowly and silently thanked Daisy for her warning. She had said that the smashed-up school was being described as a "Tiny problem –" the code she has always used to warn her little brother, Tiny, that he was about to be blamed for something. Even now, when she seemed so impossibly far away, she was keeping him out of trouble.

CHAPTER 11

TRUST AND TRUTHS

Darren rebuilt his cardboard burrow and climbed in so it covered his head. It had taken him hours to creep his way back to his arch from St Pancras. A helicopter circled overhead as the search for him continued. Voices came and went on the bridge above and even along the train tracks. The night deepened and the air grew cold. Then, as the distinctive whirr of rotor blades passed low overhead once more, Darren heard the crunch of a single pair of footsteps making its way along the edge of the nearest tracks. A figure emerged from the darkness, walking confidently despite not using a torch, and made straight for the Portakabin, where Grant, Devina and Robbie stepped out to meet him. The unknown person was at least as tall as Grant, but far thinner. Darren realized who he was just before he spoke.

"Good evening," Marek said. "I wonder if you could help me find a friend of mine. He's twelve years old and rather unique to look at."

"Sorry, mate," Robbie answered. "No kids here."

"Ah, yes," Marek agreed. "I see that, but perhaps he passed by? His name's Darren. He's rather short for his age and remarkably broad. He stands a little stooped. You know, he looks at his shoes most of the time when he walks. He's a little wild-looking and his hair is light blue."

Grant thought for a moment. "Nope."

"Are you sure?"

"I think we'd remember," Devina answered curtly.

Marek narrowed his eyes. "Just so *you* know, *I* know there is a ninety-one per cent chance *you're* lying. And *I* have ways of finding out for sure."

"No need." Darren emerged into the firelight. "They don't need you in their heads."

Marek clapped his hands with excitement. "I knew it! I knew I'd got it right this time. Darren, you really are extraordinarily hard to find!"

"Cheers," Darren answered carefully. "What have you got on your face?"

"These?" Marek pointed at the bulky goggles covering his eyes. The insect-eye style lenses created a hundred mini replicas of Marek's eyes. "State-of-the-art night vision."

"You look weird. Come over here," said Darren, leading Marek to his archway, and sitting down on his cardboard burrow. He waved away concerned expressions from the railworkers. They swapped apprehensive glances between themselves, but clearly decided to give the boys some space and looked away.

Marek sat opposite Darren, trying to find a spot that wasn't dirty. "I love what you've done with the place."

Darren ignored the comment. "What do you want, Marek?"

Marek pointed upwards as the helicopter passed overhead. "They've almost found you, you know that? There's a ring of steel round here and the train station. A police unit every fifty metres. Every exit covered with thermal imaging. And now they're moving in."

"So?"

"So, you can escape with me." Marek held up the SQUID.

Darren shook his head. "I won't go with you just because I'm scared of them."

Marek tutted. "More fool you."

"So, if they catch me, then what?"

"Come on, Darren, you know how this is going." He showed Darren his phone. "This is what they're saying about you."

Darren pretended to read the mix of shapes on Marek's

phone, then waved it away. "Whatever, Marek. If they catch me, what happens if I say you made me do it all? The school, escaping jail, everything."

Marek snorted. "You think that'll stick?"

Darren shrugged. "Maybe this guy called Marek hypnotized me. He's a manipulative psychopath who's wanted in twenty-nine countries and stuff…"

Marek removed his night-vision goggles and rubbed his eyes as understanding dawned. "They contacted you."

"Maybe."

"Miss Inghart?"

Darren nodded.

Marek smiled. "Okay, but you don't trust her either."

"No."

"Why not?"

Darren thought about explaining, but decided against it. "Just something tiny. You wouldn't understand."

Marek frowned. "Have it your own way. Don't tell me."

Voices drifted to them from the rail tracks. Darren could see shapes moving in the distance. The helicopter passed overhead again, but this time hovered for over a minute before moving on.

"There are people over there?" Marek asked.

Darren nodded.

"Do you see them yet?"

"Not properly. From the voices, I'd say ten men and two women. More a bit further away."

Marek shook his head. "I wish I had hearing like yours."

Darren scanned his surroundings for a way to escape. He could hear more people on the bridge above. Ahead of him, Devina was keeping a watchful eye on Marek while Grant and Robbie stared nervously into the darkness.

"Seems like you're going to have to decide," Marek said. "Them or me."

"No."

"We're cornered."

"I know."

"All right, you don't trust me, I get that." Marek handed Darren the SQUID. "So let's do it your way. You work out how we can escape and we escape together. It's all up to you."

"I can't use this."

"I know. I suppose you'll have to find another way."

Darren stared at Marek, wondering if he was serious.

Marek seemed to read his mind. "No games."

"Why?"

"Because there's not a human on Earth I'd trust to save me from Miss Inghart and her associates, but I trust you."

Marek's apparent faith in him made Darren uncomfortable, but he decided he must be serious. "Okay.

This doesn't mean I'm coming with you once we're safe."

"I understand. Even I can hear them now. You need to hurry."

Darren closed his eyes and let his mind drift, allowing his thoughts to dissolve into the night. The people shouting were just another sound among many: the calls and scurries of small animals; two cats circling for a fight; the crackle of the fire; the distant cars and helicopter; the slow, steady flow of a river beneath his feet...

"There's a river underneath us."

Marek raised an eyebrow. "The River Fleet, I imagine. More of a sewer these days, I think."

"It's a lot louder over here." Darren led Marek a metre or so from the arch and kicked away at the litter and weeds. A manhole cover emerged from the dirt.

Marek held his night-vision goggles to his eyes and pulled a face. "Definitely a sewer then."

Darren gripped the cover and pulled it free. The smell wasn't as bad as he'd imagined it would be.

Marek coughed. "Oh, that's gross!"

The darkness within was pitch-black even to Darren's eyes. He whistled into the hole and from the echo he could tell the space below was large. He tested a ladder that was bolted just below the hole. It seemed secure. "How good are those night-vision goggles?"

"Very."

"Okay, you first."

"Why me?"

"So I can drag the cover back in place."

"There goes another suit," Marek complained, but he slid past Darren and began descending the ladder. Darren checked that the railway workers weren't watching, all three now distracted by the approaching voices, and followed. Better, he thought, to keep them out of his troubles. He couldn't deal with them not wanting him to go with Marek when he had so little time. The moment he pulled the cover into place, all light was extinguished.

"Okay," Marek said from below him, "my goggles aren't perfect. I can't see a thing."

"Just keep going."

"Okay, okay. I'm at the bottom. Eurgh! The water's gone over the top of my shoes!"

Darren sped up, using Marek's voice as a guide, and jumped off the last rung to land beside him.

"Which way?" Marek asked.

"North," Darren answered.

"How can you be sure which way's north?"

"I'm always sure."

"That's useful."

It would be if I could read a map, Darren thought to himself.

To Marek he just said, "Yeah," and then started along a narrow walkway that ran against the wall just above the height of the water, using his sensitive ears to guide them. They travelled in single file with Darren leading and Marek following with one hand on his shoulder. The only sounds were their footsteps, the trickling of water and Marek muttering to himself.

Eventually, Marek gripped his shoulder tighter. "I need a rest."

They walked about another thirty metres until Darren felt an alcove in the tunnel. He sat down and watched Marek use the light of his phone to pick the least dirty spot of ground to do the same. Then Marek pulled out what looked like a large marble and placed it on the ground between them.

Darren eyed the marble suspiciously. "Is that going to blow up?"

Marek tapped his phone screen. "No. Much as I trust you to lead me through this darkness, I just need some light so I can see you while we rest." The marble began to glow. It spread a pale light in a fifty centimetre radius, illuminating the red Victorian brickwork of the sewer and a couple of rats, who immediately dived into the water and out of sight. "According to my phone, we've gone a couple of kilometres in ninety minutes. I hope that puts us outside the ring of steel."

"Okay," Darren answered.

"So, while we wait, what did Miss Inghart say about me?" Marek asked.

"That they've realized it was all really you. That she's with the police who are chasing you."

"That's convenient," Marek commented sarcastically.

"That you hypnotized me into smashing up my school and all the rest."

"You know I can't do that."

"Do I?"

"Humans practically hypnotize themselves, but you perceive the world in a different way, just like dogs smell the world and cats hear the world in different ways – and I can't hypnotize those species either."

"So I'm a dog now?"

Marek rolled his large eyes. "Listen to what I'm *actually* saying. Why would I tell you everything, about you and me, if I could just hypnotize you?"

"Maybe you had your reasons."

Marek huffed in frustration. "Why would I get you into huge trouble by destroying your school if I could just make you do what I wanted from the start? You'd be a lot more use to me as an anonymous twelve-year-old, wouldn't you?"

Darren stayed quiet, looking for something in Marek's face to trust.

Marek continued. "Come on, Darren! You want to think for yourself, so think! When Miss Inghart was chasing you across that roof, did she seem like some regular cop?"

"No," Darren admitted.

"Why would she be interested in you if she's supposed to be looking for a psychopath like me?"

Darren thought for a while. He had to admit that Marek was making sense. He quietly thanked Daisy for her warning. "So I don't believe Miss Inghart. How do I know I can trust you?"

Marek didn't react at all to Darren's question. He simply sat in total silence, almost statue-like. Darren got a sense that Marek was thinking deeply, in a different way from his usual remarkably rapid thought processes. Marek's angled eyelids blinked once into the V-shape Darren found familiar, and then he spoke in a way that made it clear that he shouldn't be interrupted. "You like music, don't you, Darren? I saw you in the van, moving this way and that when the radio was on. You seem to get a lot out of it. Enjoyment...comfort...whatever. I don't know how that feels." He paused and cast a four-thumbed shadow by placing his hands over the marble. "I have my theories. I think maybe my alien ancestors came from a planet with a thin atmosphere where sound doesn't travel well, you see. Or maybe they just had different ways to communicate.

That would make sense too." He paused again and his free hand drifted protectively to one of his tiny ears. "I can't hear music. It just sounds like noise to me – a big horrible mess of sound. I can tell someone's singing because their voice sounds different, but if there's a tune, I don't hear it. I don't feel it. My brain just isn't wired that way."

Marek lapsed into silence. The admission seemed to have taken a huge effort.

Darren leaned forward. "What, you don't hear tunes at all?"

Marek shook his head and in the half-light he seemed to blush. "I can see that there are beautiful patterns in music if I analyse it on a computer, but I can't even clap in time to a nursery rhyme."

"Wow."

"Wow indeed," Marek agreed. "I've set my phone up to tell me if music is playing and what kind. It tells me if it is energetic or sad or whatever. It helps me hide my problem." He sighed. "You see, I'm used to looking different and eating differently and noticing how people react to that. I'm used to everyone knowing I'm cleverer than they are the moment I speak. I even *like* that most of the time. I like how I can think and what I can see with these strange eyes of mine, attuned to ultraviolet light, but I've never told anyone about the music."

"Why not?"

"Because I feel stupid." Marek shuddered. "I don't want to admit that I, Marek Masters, the most intelligent being on the planet, have to live with this stupid, stupid weakness. But I can tell *you*, I think. Maybe you can understand."

Darren let Marek's words sink in. The idea of a world without music seemed strange and somehow scary to him. Music formed a soundtrack to his life, giving him a sense of the mood and time of each memory. It expressed the feelings he couldn't express himself. He thought of all the nights his music had kept him company and kept him part of the world when everything else felt detached or distant. He felt a surge of sympathy for Marek. Watching him in the marble's weak light, he could see that the part-alien boy was tired. Physically, yes, but emotionally as well. His admission had drained him, on top of whatever else he was dealing with.

Darren listened to the trickle of water and the occasional squeak of a rat and felt a truth he would rather keep to himself climbing its way up from the dark pit of his soul and into his throat until it reached his lips.

"I can't read," he said, and was surprised to hear how emotional his voice sounded. He cleared his throat. "I see words on a page, but they're just shapes and squiggles to me. People say that this one's an A or that one's a B, but I don't get how they can be a shape and also something else. I can't write either. Not even my name. People say you can learn to write your name without knowing what the shapes mean, but…I don't know."

Marek tipped his head. "But your brain isn't wired that way."

Darren shook his head. "No, it isn't." He felt strangely exposed as Marek watched him – it was the same way he felt whenever he came out of a good hiding place. He looked away from Marek, to hide the emotions he feared were playing on his face.

"I knew you'd understand," Marek said. "You know, maybe I do like being different most of the time, but I didn't choose it. I can't ever choose to be normal even for a single minute of a single day of my entire life." His expression hardened. "I am going to make Project Helix pay for what they did to me."

The intensity of Marek's words made Darren rock back slightly. He understood, more deeply than he knew how to say, what Marek meant about not having a choice about being different, and about feeling stupid. As he watched Marek's very certain, defiant expression, he was gripped by a completely different desire.

"I just want to go home."

Marek looked off into the darkness as he considered

Darren's response. "Well, Darren. If we work together, as equals in our very different ways, perhaps we can both get what we want."

Darren found that he wasn't ready to answer, so instead he smelled the air. "I think there's a way up further along."

Marek got up slowly and extinguished the light. "Lead the way."

With some difficulty, Darren pushed at the underside of a manhole cover to lift it and peered out into a deserted park. The night seemed light compared to the tunnel and Darren could see clearly to the park's edge. He climbed out, pulled Marek after him and then replaced the cover.

"Any idea where this is?"

Marek checked his phone. "Caledonian Park. You were right. We went north."

Darren looked around and saw an old clock tower. "Hop on."

He waited for Marek to do as he asked. Then he lolloped across the open ground, leaped onto the tower wall and began to climb. Marek gave a yelp as Darren jumped but then gripped tighter and remained silent until they reached a balcony just below the clock bells.

Once they were safely behind the balcony railings,

Marek scanned the sky. "Seems like the helicopter's gone." He looked south through his goggles. "I think I see St Pancras. Let me check the exact coordinates. Yes…we're outside their security cordon." He looked at Darren, his odd-shaped head framed by the Milky Way. "Well done. You escaped without the need for my technology, just as I trusted you would."

Darren handed him back the SQUID. "Cheers." He looked out over London and knew, deep down, that it was only a temporary escape.

Marek was now staring at him expectantly. He knew it was impossible to consider Marek's offer of working together without also thinking about the consequences – if he didn't agree – of trying to survive alone in London. In the end, it didn't matter how well he hid, tunnelled and climbed, somebody – the police or Miss Inghart – would find him.

"I need time to think," he said finally.

"I see." Marek pulled what looked like a small torch on a key ring from a pocket. "In that case, please take this."

"What is it?"

"A mini-SQUID. It doesn't have much battery charge, so its range is very limited. It can only manage three short-range trips. I have programmed it with our DNA, so only you or I can use it." Marek showed Darren the shaft.

"See the red light? Activate by pressing the keychain end and the dimensional gateway will appear."

"You mean the swirl of colours?"

"Yes. The light goes amber while the gateway stabilizes. Wait till the light goes green and you can go through. Turn as you enter so that the SQUID is the last thing to pass through on the other side. Then switch it off."

"Um…how do I tell it where I need to go?"

"I'm afraid you can't. That is immensely complicated. I'll have to program in both your start and finish coordinates. You'll only be able to use it to travel between two places. That's all. One end will be my home. The other you can choose."

"Anywhere I choose?"

"Anywhere within ten miles of here."

Darren thought. "My archway then."

"The archway it is." Marek tapped his phone. "Programming complete. Here." He handed Darren the mini-SQUID. "If you decide to come, use it to join me. If you decide not to, crush it. I'll know and I won't ever bother you again."

Darren accepted the mini-SQUID. "Okay."

Marek smiled. "Think of it as a spare key for a welcome guest who may come and go as he pleases." He produced his own SQUID and shone a disc of colour in the air just beyond the balcony. "Till, hopefully, we meet again," he said and climbed onto the railing.

"Hey, Marek," Darren called. "If you had that mini-SQUID with you the whole time – down in the sewer, you didn't need to trust me to escape."

Marek laughed as he disappeared through the swirling disc. "You see, I do listen to you. This time, I had a Plan B!"

Darren spent the daylight hours back down in the sewer, letting everything that had happened since the day he'd smashed up his school swirl around his head like shipwreck debris in the ocean. Slowly, in the safety of the dark, he sorted lies from truth as best he could, and things he understood from those he didn't. Options, with their pros and cons, surfaced in his mind. Some floated better on the ocean than others. Eventually, only one remained.

He waited until his instincts told him it was dark and then climbed from the sewer back into his archway. He watched Robbie, Grant and Devina build another fire and decided not to speak to them. The less they knew, he felt, the safer they would be.

He shone the mini-SQUID at the arch wall and watched the disc form. It was smaller than Marek's, but high enough for Darren. He stepped towards it and waited as the light shone amber.

There was a question he had to ask Marek and then, depending on his answer, a promise Marek needed to make if Darren was going to join him. Darren wondered, apprehensively, how that conversation would go.

The light turned green. Marek had called the mini-SQUID a spare key. As he walked and turned his spare key into the gateway, Darren thought wryly that it seemed a lot more like a cat flap for the pet he suspected Marek had once hoped he'd be. Darren passed through the swirling disc of colours and found himself in a brightly-lit room. The walls were made of cool, featureless metal on all three sides he could see. He switched off the mini-SQUID and turned to find Marek standing, with a broad grin on his face, in front of a large, open, metal door. The door was more than a metre thick and had the kind of circular handle that you normally saw on a bank vault.

Marek followed Darren's gaze. "Oh, I know. This used to be a nuclear bunker before the army decommissioned it in the 1990s and buried the entrance under metres of concrete. They weren't big into underground chic, but hey…one person's underground lair is another man's Batcave, right? Come on in!" He turned to walk through the door.

Darren didn't move. "I've got a question."

Marek rolled his eyes as he turned back. "I should have known."

Darren breathed in deeply and placed a finger on the mini-SQUID in case he got the answer he expected but didn't want. "Have you ever killed anyone?"

"No," Marek answered with complete certainty.

Instinctively, Darren knew he was telling the truth. He felt a flood of relief and pocketed the mini-SQUID. "Good."

Then Marek frowned thoughtfully. "Although, to be honest, that's more by luck than judgement."

Darren fixed him with an intense yellow-eyed stare. "If you ever kill anyone, we're done. You understand?"

"What, anybody?"

"Anybody. No second chances. If you kill, I leave."

"Even if they're trying to kill us?"

"Especially if they're trying to kill us."

Marek gave Darren a pleading look. "Seriously?"

"Yes."

Marek tapped the thumbs of his right hand together thoughtfully. "That would make bringing down a secret international organization most likely responsible for a scientific conspiracy that killed almost fifty innocent children practically impossible."

Darren nodded. "Yeah, but you're the cleverest guy on the planet."

"True…"

"So it should be easy for you."

Marek's face worked hard. "Appealing, I admit, but… no, it would be like painting a masterpiece without the colour red. Unnecessarily difficult."

"I dare you."

"Oh, you *dare* me?" Marek's large eyes narrowed to two angled slits. He considered Darren carefully. "Okay, it's a deal!" He walked forwards and extended a hand.

Darren grinned and shook it. "Right then, now you can show me around."

CHAPTER 12

GOING DARK

Marek's bunker turned out to be a maze of corridors leading off from a central hexagonal area. Each exit from the central area was a different colour, marked in age-flecked paint which then continued down the corridors beyond. After wandering around listening to Marek's constant chatter and dodging various small robots scuttling about as they carried out chores, Darren came to understand that this was deliberate coding.

Green took you to military barracks for the soldiers who would have lived there after a nuclear strike.

Yellow was for food storage and preparation.

Blue led to construction, maintenance and weaponry areas.

White included administration, laundry and medical.

Orange was for decontamination and access to the outside world.

Only the red exit didn't lead to a maze of corridors. This led directly to the Command and Control centre. It was here that Marek finished the tour.

He pointed to a bank of TV screens that covered three walls. "Over there, I monitor social media. That's how I found you, by the way – when you had your school-destroying monster moment."

"Don't call it that, please."

Marek shrugged. "As you wish. Anyway, beside that are screens showing news outlets. BBC, CNN and so on. Then here I monitor law-enforcement communications. The Metropolitan Police, MI5 and 6, FBI, Interpol, the Russian FSB, the Chinese Armed Police Force, and so on. Front and centre is the world map where I track military movements and anything I pick up about our friends at Project Helix from my other monitoring. They are very sneaky."

Darren looked at the different coloured dots all over the map. "How can you know it's them?"

"Because I'm the most intelligent person who has ever lived. Even so, it's like chasing smoke." He pointed to the next screen. "Over here is my monitoring of London above us. Then I monitor criminal activity and major spy organizations on these screens – strictly professional interest, you understand. I have to make a living and this kit is expensive. Finally, down here on the table I play chess and oversee automated construction of innovative items." He swept a hand towards a large oval table covered in various partly-constructed gadgets and a neatly arranged chess set. "A SQUID doesn't invent itself, after all, and even I have to relax. Make sense?"

"Yes," Darren lied.

"Good, good… Well, listen, I'm a bit behind on a few things. Are you okay to keep looking around? Choose wherever you want to sleep. Try not to step on any of the bots with those big feet of yours. Otto has already complained."

After wandering around the bunker for a while, Darren settled on the infirmary as a place to live. The nurse's room was smaller than the open bunk areas he'd found in the living quarters and felt safer. There was also a shower and a small kitchen that was more manageable than the industrial-sized kitchen in the yellow zone. He dragged a bed into what was now his room and set about building a den in which to sleep while hidden from the world. There was, of course, nothing to hide from in the bunker except for Marek's small robots, which rolled and skittered about the place. However, the whole bunker had a feeling that Darren didn't much like. The quiet echo of every sound and the weak electric lighting gave the place an eerie quality that put him on edge.

The best moments of Darren's first few days in the bunker were the hot showers and finding a supply of steaks in the yellow zone that Marek had acquired for his arrival, along with some spare military uniforms that fitted him well once he'd torn off the bottoms of the trouser legs. The worst moments were in the hours when he lay wide awake in his den, instinctively knowing that it was night-time in the world above, despite the bunker's eerie glow that never ceased due to Marek's poor night vision and habit of working through both day and night. Then his thoughts would wander to Farlington and the hollow feeling in his heart would grow more intense as he thought of his mum, dad and especially Daisy. He thought of the pain and worry he must be causing them and he thought about his school, now destroyed thanks to what Marek had flippantly called his "monster moment". Darren's memory swirled around his dad's words – *"please come home"*. He couldn't get his head around the fact that it had become so hard, so dangerous, so impossible to do that one simple thing.

In the end, after days alone with the same swirl of thoughts and memories, Darren got angry with himself.

He was gripped with a need to do something, *anything*, to change his situation – even if it risked making things worse.

He lolloped towards the red zone, making the robots dodge and skitter out of his way, and came to a halt at the entrance. Marek was working, just as he had been every time Darren had seen him since he arrived. His shirtsleeves were neatly rolled to the elbow and his jacket and tie lay folded on a chair. His concentration was so intense that he didn't notice Darren at the entrance, just as he hadn't on previous occasions.

"Marek!" Darren called.

Marek didn't respond. His attention flicked back and forth between the map of the world and his social-media screens, his hands flitting across several keyboards.

Darren called again. "Marek?"

Marek turned his attention to his law-enforcement screens.

Darren tapped his foot impatiently. "Marek…Marek… Marek…Marek… Marek…Marek…Marek…MAREK!"

Marek turned towards him and slowly focused on him as though he was waking up from a dream. "Hmmm? Oh, Darren. You're out of hiding then?"

"Yeah."

Marek smiled. "Excellent. Is there something you need? The bots can get most things." He pointed to a metre-high robot composed of a double camera set on the end of a mechanical arm attached to tracked wheels. "I can ask Marvin to be your personal servant, if you like."

"No, I don't need one."

"Okay," Marek said, and glanced longingly at his screens, as though the few seconds of tearing his attention away from them had been painful. "I suppose that means you want to talk?"

"No," Darren said flatly, "I want to do something."

"Do something?"

"Yeah, take down Project Helix or something," Darren clarified.

Marek raised an eyebrow. "Or something?"

"Anything."

Marek's eyes narrowed as he considered Darren's words. "Darren, I'm sensing frustration." He sighed and pointed to his screens. "Sadly, they've gone dark."

"Dark?"

"Yes, the organization behind Project Helix, whoever they are," Marek explained. "I've been tracking them for two years, but now, since your escape from Miss Inghart, they've stopped all activity across seven continents. As I said, completely dark."

"Why would they do that?"

"I'm not sure... I've been interfering with their operations for the past couple of years, just generally causing them trouble. I put a few agents' faces on conspiracy-theory websites so they had to be withdrawn from undercover operations. I've called in anonymous tips to local police and journalists. That kind of thing. I've been trying to lure them out, make them attack me. People are always most vulnerable when they attack – that's when I find out useful information. But now there's nothing. Absolutely nothing..." Marek stared at his screens apprehensively. "Maybe I'm missing something."

"So what do we do?"

Marek shook his head and remained silent as he continued to study the streams of information in front of him. Eventually, he turned back to Darren. "For now, nothing."

Darren's frustration bubbled into his words. "What, so we just stay down here?"

Marek frowned. "Darren, it could take a long time to defeat this organization. I never said it would be quick. They are incredibly secretive."

"But I need to *do* something."

Marek thought for a moment and seemed to come to a decision. "Well, I can keep an eye on things from my phone." He smiled at Darren. "How would you like to do some experiments?"

Darren frowned. "I'm not good at science."

Marek shook his head. "Oh no, I'd be the one doing the experimenting. I'd like to find out more about you."

Darren pulled a face. "You want to experiment *on* me?"

Marek lifted a pacifying hand. "Oh, don't worry. It wouldn't be anything too probing."

"What kind of things?"

"Well, I'd like to understand your abilities better. How fast you are, how strong, more about your monstrous instincts. I'd especially like to X-ray your body and scan your brain. I want to understand in exactly what ways you are monstrous."

Darren shifted uncomfortably. "I dunno."

Marek smiled. "Listen, I've only been able to find out snippets of information about our parentage from my hacking. I've had to work the rest out. I won't ask you to do anything I wouldn't do myself. I've experimented on my own body extensively and, I assure you, I'm still in one piece. I've been trying to work out what kind of planet my alien parentage comes from, you see. I think it must have low gravity, as that would explain my low bone density and height. I also think it may have many moons. That would make the nights bright, which is why I can't see in the dark. Low gravity and many moons reflecting light would also mean a lot of UV light getting to the surface. Hence, I can see in the UV spectrum. So who knows what I can find out about you with a little light experimentation…"

Darren considered Marek's offer. The idea that it was something Marek was happy to do to himself wasn't particularly reassuring. "I'm here to take down Project Helix so I can go home. Not to do experiments."

Marek nodded. "True, but it would help me understand what you are capable of before we go on missions to take down Project Helix, so we can both get what we want."

Darren shook his head. "But I already know what I can do."

Marek laughed. "I very much doubt that, Darren. You've spent your life dealing with what you *can't* do. Perhaps it's time to discover just how much you *can*? After all, being different is what makes us special." He raised an arm. "For example, if I hadn't experimented on myself, I never would have discovered how well designed my hands are. We are trained by everyday life to accept certain things as normal, like having four fingers and a thumb, but there are always exceptions."

Marek picked up a wire. "My hands are not human hands with an extra thumb instead of a little finger. They are achiral dipollex xenoappendages. Although 'twin-thumbed hand' might be easier to remember. It is a different design that works perfectly well in its own way. Just as a cat's paw is different to an eagle's claw, my alien hands have their own strengths. Can 'normal' people do this?"

Marek gripped each end of the wire with a different thumb and finger of his right hand, used his free middle finger to press the wire to his palm and proceeded to tie a neat bow one-handed.

Darren couldn't help but be impressed. "That's quality."

Marek smiled. "Indeed it is. Darren, you are potentially far more extraordinary than you realize. We just have to understand what you are designed to do."

"I'm not extraordinary."

"You don't know that, Darren. I don't know that. We won't unless I experiment."

Darren shuffled nervously and fought the urge to hide under the table. "Then we go on missions?"

"Then we go on missions," Marek confirmed.

"To take down Project Helix?"

"I promise."

Darren grinned through his nervousness. "Okay."

CHAPTER 13

MONSTROUS TENDENCIES

Miss Inghart ducked her head and entered the tunnel that ran under the Ministry of Justice. The dry air felt chilly against her skin, making her shiver. After three hundred metres, she came to a door that opened automatically for her. She pulled her hair into a tight ponytail and checked her suit jacket, readying herself to face the video screen she knew would be inside.

She entered and drew in a sharp breath. Someone was standing inside the otherwise empty room.

"Good afternoon, Miss Inghart."

"Mrs Lahaine, what are you doing here?"

Mrs Lahaine raised a single critical eyebrow that made Miss Inghart squirm. "All XSP communications are on black. Verbal only. I had little choice. The General doesn't even know I'm here."

"I'm sorry, you just took me by surprise."

"I don't expect my agents to be taken by surprise," Mrs Lahaine answered witheringly.

Miss Inghart started to answer, but then decided it was safer not to.

Mrs Lahaine continued. "I'm under immense pressure to end the operations blackout. It is costing me huge personal credibility. The Council is not happy. There's more to what we do than catching Masters and Devlin, even if they turn out to be as valuable or dangerous together as we suspect. There are important elections in seven large countries within the next year to manipulate, and major movement by one of our enemies in South East Asia and the USA. We can't afford to be in hiding for long."

"I realize that, Mrs Lahaine, but I know I'm right."

Mrs Lahaine didn't look impressed. "I need more than your self-confidence to keep this going."

"Ma'am, I know Marek. I watched him play chess online against the best players in the world thousands of times. I even saw him play twelve grandmasters at once, at the age of six, when we pretended he was a new supercomputer. He never lost."

"I'm aware of this, Miss Inghart!"

She ploughed on. "But he always wanted to play black. Never white. It's supposed to be easier to win if you play white because you go first, but Marek found it harder. It took him an average of seven moves longer to win when he played white. Marek likes to understand your strategy. Then he draws you in and destroys you. So we remain on black. We don't do anything. In the end, he'll get frustrated and make the first move. That's when he's vulnerable. That's how we beat him."

Mrs Lahaine picked up her briefcase. "Very well, but it isn't only Marek who is getting frustrated. When you and Mr Ducas briefed us just weeks ago, it was made clear by Councillor Eight that trust in you was almost at an end. I would say that now – how might the General put it? – you are a plane flying on fumes. I need results – *something* – or I will be forced to cut you loose."

Miss Inghart nodded. "I understand."

Mrs Lahaine's expression hardened. She walked past Miss Inghart towards the tunnel. The door opened. "You don't get to retire from XSP, Miss Inghart. When this is done, either you or Masters will be in a coffin."

Darren lay in the MRI scanner's small white tunnel and tried to ignore the sound of the machine's huge electromagnet, which was close to deafening despite the noise-cancelling headphones Marek had given him.

Marek's voice crackled through the headphones. "Okay, next test! These images of your brain are remarkable!"

Darren groaned. After days of experiments, he was deeply regretting agreeing to Marek's suggestion. For the first test, he had been tasked with hiding from Marvin the robot. This had been fun to begin with, but Marvin had become increasingly good at finding him, which soon became really irritating. He'd taken to hiding high up, where he assumed the track-wheeled robot would not be able to follow, only to find that it had suckers to drive up walls. It always ended up staring at him with its large double camera in a way that somehow managed to look incredibly smug. Eventually, Darren had hidden Marvin in a bin and refused to give him back unless they moved on to a different experiment.

That had led to another brief moment of fun, when Marek had given him a break and SQUIDed them into his favourite clothes shop on Savile Row. There, a hypnotized tailor had measured Darren in every direction. Darren had found this a bit embarrassing, but he'd managed to sneak out while Marek was checking out the latest fashions and lolloped to a park nearby, where he'd swung from tree to tree until Marek had caught up with him.

Marek had placed both hands on his hips. "Darren Devlin, will you come here this minute? You're acting like that out-of-control pet you didn't want to be!"

Darren had reluctantly returned underground, but next Marek had arranged for him to tackle a range of assault courses in near-total darkness. It had felt good to climb and run, even if it was within the compact space of the bunker.

The past two days, however, had all been devoted to X-rays and MRI scans.

Both nights they'd SQUIDed into St Bernard's Hospital to use the equipment. Both mornings, Darren had arrived back at the bunker with a headache and a ringing in his ears from the noise of the giant machine. Even worse, he'd had to put up with doing a range of irritating tasks set by Marek while lying in the scanner. These involved everything from correctly identifying pictures and sounds to saying certain sentences over and over again, which was fine for a while, but Darren was less keen on having his feet prodded with a set of cocktail sticks. Marek had only stopped when Darren had threatened to put a cocktail stick somewhere painful.

The current night's events had proved even stranger. Marek had mainly been fiddling with the machine's air conditioning. Darren had been subjected to sudden blasts of warm or cold air. Now he waited, dreading what Marek would do next, while wondering if his hearing would ever recover.

Marek's shadow loomed at the tunnel entrance. "Don't move," he ordered.

Chance would be a fine thing, Darren thought irritably.

A spray of cold water hit him in the face. He spluttered and crawled out to find Marek standing by the scanner. He had a joyful grin on his face and was carrying a small fire extinguisher.

"Perfect!" he said cheerily. "That'll give me some great data!"

Darren wiped his face with his jumper. He swiped the extinguisher from Marek. "Remember what I said about the cocktail stick?"

Marek gulped. "I'm sensing your patience with the MRI is running out?"

"With all of it!"

"Ah." Marek twiddled his long thumbs. "I see. Hmmm…" He eyed Darren. "So, we're done?"

"Yup."

"For now?"

"For ever!"

Marek sighed with disappointment and pulled the SQUID from his pocket. "Very well."

Back at the bunker, Darren made for his room and hid in his burrow. His irritation began to subside as his hearing returned and he started to feel bad about shouting at Marek.

He sighed and went to the Command and Control centre, pausing at the entrance.

He watched Marek's attention flit between screens as the images changed rapidly. Watching him, Darren began to get a sense of just how attuned to the screens Marek was. He worked with multiple computers like a cross between an orchestra conductor and a spider at the centre of a web. They reacted to him as though they were all part of a living thing with Marek as the brain. Marek had once told Darren that he had an IQ of two hundred and ninety-nine, but now Darren realized that this part-alien boy was intelligent in ways a human test couldn't hope to measure.

"Sorry," he called, "about shouting."

Marek turned towards him and placed a hand over his heart. "I admit, I may have got a little carried away. It's just that you are so very interesting." He paused and searched Darren's face. "However, I'm guessing further experiments really are off the menu?"

"I'll smash up the next MRI I see."

Marek nodded and beckoned. "Understood. Come in, please. I may as well show you what I've found out about you."

Feeling suddenly apprehensive, Darren walked in while Marek cleared the world map from the central screen. He sat on a vacant chair as Marek lined up some files.

"So," Marek began, "the first thing to say is that it's hard to measure your monstrous qualities. The information I have been able to find has some very frustrating gaps, even after our experimentation. The Project Helix file I hacked before I found you just lists the DNA they hid in the food as 'genetic code: monster' and the DNA sample is incomplete. The file only refers to 'identified monstrous tendencies' and is vague about exactly what those tendencies are. I can't tell what long-dead monstrous creature they've got locked in a vault somewhere, along with my alien parent. But I can tell that the DNA is ancient, probably belonging to an extinct creature from the time of the sabre-toothed tiger. That's not much to go on, though, and whatever it is certainly isn't known to modern science."

"Monstrous tendencies…" Darren repeated. There was a strange feeling in his stomach as he thought of some dangerous creature locked away somewhere. Now its DNA was locked inside him. He shivered. "Go on."

Marek continued. "I therefore compared your instincts and abilities to other alpha predators." He grinned excitedly. "Believe me, Darren, I'd do a drum roll if I knew how. You share a lot of qualities with this big fellow."

Darren looked at the picture Marek brought up on screen. "A grizzly bear?"

Marek nodded. "Cool or what? You share its immense

physical strength and its speed over a short distance. You have an excellent sense of smell and strong night vision, just like the grizzly. You also prefer to hide or roar if confronted. However, if you have to attack –" he let a video play of a bear charging – "I think this speaks for itself."

Darren watched the bear making a lolloping attack on a group of fleeing tourists, who piled into a car just before the bear rammed into it. He remembered how Daisy had always likened him to the bear in her favourite picture book. He smiled. It turned out she'd been right. It was, he had to admit, a pretty cool animal to be similar to.

Marek brought up a photo of another bear species. "Your climbing ability is more like the smaller black bear. As you can see, they can pretty much run up a tree. Your eyes are interesting. When I squirted water on your face, the scan showed an extra lens sliding across your eyes. Polar bears have the same adaptation. It lets them see clearly underwater when they swim. I'm guessing you see well underwater?"

"Doesn't everyone?"

Marek shook his head. "No, they don't. That's why they wear goggles."

"I thought that was because of the chlorine," Darren explained as he watched a video of a polar bear swimming through the Arctic Ocean.

"I assume you're good at swimming?"

Darren shrugged. His style was a doggy paddle that looked strangely like the bear's in the video. His swimming teacher had always told him off for not using proper swimming strokes, but it was true Darren was fast.

"I do okay," he admitted.

Marek clapped his hands as the screen cleared, then filled up again with various complex medical diagrams of animals. "I'll test that when you let me. Anyway, you may have many bearlike qualities, but you're no bear. Your hearing is utterly fascinating." He brought up images of Darren's brain. "Vast areas of your brain respond to sound. You seem to be able to hear the whole area around you in huge detail, like a black bear. However, you also have hearing abilities similar to this gentleman." Marek opened a picture of an owl.

Darren looked unconvinced. "How am I like a bird?"

"Owls have a way of filtering sound," Marek explained. "They can pick out a mouse's heartbeat over the noise of a herd of cows. It is a highly honed predatory sense. You too have the ability to pick out a single noise, and you appear to be able to choose, at least subconsciously, which sound to follow."

Darren let this news sink in. "Cool!"

"It is, isn't it?" Marek agreed. "There are other things

I don't understand yet. Why you always know which way is north, for example, and why you seem to always know if it's day or night even when we're down here. There is something going on with your sense of touch as well. Your brain responds to touch in a completely different way to any species on record I can find. I'm just not sure why yet. I think it is all linked and might explain why you are so good at hiding. Then there's those strangely hard nails of yours."

Darren looked down at his short, dark nails. "Mum's always complaining she can't cut them."

Marek smiled. "I'm not surprised. I imagine you'd need an industrial cutter."

"I bite them."

"A lovely image. Hard blunt nails and big hands... As I said, I'm sure it's all linked."

Darren thought for a moment. "That's all cool and everything..."

"But?" Marek asked.

"But it's not very monstery," Darren said, shrugging. "I mean, what am I?"

Marek grinned excitedly. "I know, and I don't have all the answers, but something struck me when I first met you. Something about your eyes was unnerving for no reason I could explain." He brought up dozens of pictures on screen.

Most were old drawings and paintings of the kind you'd see in dusty fairy-tale books or in museums. They showed werewolves, trolls and imaginary monsters of all shapes and sizes. Marek approached the screen. "Myths and stories from all over the world tell of monsters that hide in dark places and erupt with rage when they are cornered or attacked." He smiled excitedly. "Each of these drawings is from a different part of the world. The artists never knew about each other's work and none of them had seen whatever animal Project Helix used. But do you see the similarity in the eyes? They drew straight from their imaginations, but the eyes are so like yours!"

Darren shifted uneasily. "I don't understand."

"Instinct," Marek answered with a dramatic wave of a hand. "There's a reason why children have a natural instinct to be afraid of certain animals. With spiders and snakes it's because some are deadly poisonous. In just the same way, every child knows not to look in the wardrobe or under the bed after the lights go out – because if you happen to see a pair of yellow eyes staring back and if you happen to scream…well, you might not live to see the morning."

Darren's eyes drifted over each picture. There was something both familiar and unnerving about the twisted faces and…yes…he recognized the eyes from his own reflection. Deep inside him, vague memories of his moments of rage crawled out from where they were hiding: the moments when he hadn't kept the monster in the bottle.

"Turn it off, Marek."

"Why?"

"Turn it off!"

"Okay, okay… There." Marek turned to him, a puzzled look on his face. "Aren't you pleased to know more about yourself?"

Darren ran a hand over his face to give himself time to answer. "All this was so we could go on a mission, remember? To take down Project Helix."

"Mission? Oh yes, right. I think I have something that will help. Come with me!"

Darren followed Marek as he walked to the green zone.

"Remember those games of hide-and-seek you played with Marvin?" Marek asked as they walked.

"How could I forget?"

"You probably noticed that Marvin got pretty good at finding you."

"Yeah, I noticed," Darren answered grumpily.

"You are exceptional, of course. Much like a bear, you can hide in very little cover right by someone and they won't see you. You are so in tune with your surroundings, you blend in, but evolution hasn't kept up with technology.

Marvin found you using low-frequency infrared and localized radar technology."

"I've no idea what those things are."

Marek shook his head as they stopped at the laundry. "It doesn't matter. The point is that the organization behind Project Helix could work out a way to find you too. So I thought you could do with a new suit."

Darren looked doubtfully at Marek's jacket, tie and waistcoat. "A suit?"

Marek laughed and gripped the edge of a tablecloth that was draped over something beside him. "Oh, don't worry. I think we both agree that my kind of sophisticated look isn't for you. No, I thought this might be more your style."

He whipped off the cloth with a flourish. Underneath was a mannequin wearing a pair of combat trousers and a hooded jacket. Both were made out of the same fabric with a white, grey and black camouflage print.

Darren tipped his head. "Camo? Okay, cool."

"Try them on! Try them on!" Marek said, bouncing up and down with excitement.

Darren did as he was asked and was soon standing in front of a mirror. He had to admit, Marek had done a pretty good job.

"This is fine," he said.

Marek grinned. "Oh, you haven't seen the half of it!

Watch." He pressed a button on Darren's collar. The fabric immediately turned green to match the walls.

"Okay, now that really is cool," Darren admitted.

Marek's grin widened. "I designed them using stealth fabric. The clothes absorb light, radar and electromagnetic waves and then emit them. It means you blend into the background even when you're up against high-tech sensor equipment. Your signature is on average ninety-one per cent weaker than it is without the suit."

"So I'm kind of invisible?"

"Not quite," Marek warned. "If you are still, the suit works almost perfectly. If you move, you still need to be careful. A normal human, who can't stay still even when they try, would be hard to spot. *You* will be like darkness in the night. I think you could break into any top-secret facility with this on."

"Breaking in? Is that what we're doing?"

Marek waved the question away. "Hang on! I'm not finished. The fabric is also kinetically responsive."

"You're going to explain that, right?"

Marek punched the jacket. Darren felt the fabric harden. "The harder you hit it, the stiffer it gets. It uses the kinetic energy of whatever hits it to tighten up. It'll probably deflect a bullet – except at close range. I can't promise you won't get a bruise, of course. No protection is perfect."

Darren nodded appreciatively. "Bendy body armour. Nice."

Marek grinned. "My genius doesn't end there! Here – the boots are lighter than they look and the soles are made from the same material used in professional rock-climbing shoes. There's also one hundred pounds hidden under the left insole in case of emergencies. The T-shirt is one of a few I thought you'd like to wear underneath to make the outfit look normal. I'm not familiar with 'punk' bands, but I noticed you wearing a similar one in a photo when I hacked your father's social media."

Darren held up the T-shirt and grinned. It looked like an *Anarchy in the UK* original. "Good choice, Marek!" He pushed his feet into the boots and pulled the T-shirt on, before looking in the mirror. He looked every inch the young punk with wild blue hair, T-shirt and camo. He grinned. "This, I like!"

Marek placed one hand on his shoulder and surveyed his work with satisfaction. "You're welcome. After all, every gentleman needs a good tailor. Get some rest now. We can talk missions this evening once you've slept the day away."

As night fell in London far above, Darren returned to the Command and Control centre to find Marek sitting at the table in front of a pile of metal and wire. Three small robots on the table were busying themselves carrying or working on bits of tech. Darren watched as Marek examined a metal tube he was holding between the thumbs of his left hand. He was wearing a pair of glasses that hugely amplified his eyes.

"Honestly, Otto, I can't always be fixing these for you." He glanced at a six-legged mini-robot as he worked on the tube until a bright green laser sprang from it and cut a hole in a sheet of metal on the table. "There's no point being artificially intelligent if you worry about getting it wrong. Remember, failure is the stepping stone to success." He carefully passed the laser-tube back to Otto. "There you go. Don't ask me again."

The robot accepted the tube, scuttled crablike to the edge of the table and fell off. Its legs unfolded in mid-air and linked together to form a beach-ball shape. It left the Command and Control centre in four bounces, then converted back to its crab-walk and disappeared out of sight.

Marek took off his glasses and spotted Darren. He seemed nervous. "I've been hoping all day that I might find a reason not to do this, but I see no other way. It really is the only option we have."

"Do what? And why's it so bad?" Darren asked.

Marek watched him for a while before explaining. "Because they want me to do it. They're just waiting for me to make my move, but we're going to have to visit a farmhouse."

Darren felt his apprehension rise. "Why?"

Marek looked just as apprehensive as he answered: "It was my childhood home."

CHAPTER 14

THE SUPER SQUID

Darren followed Marek to the bunker's blue section, where row upon row of unused rifle racks lined the corridors leading to the vast, empty ammunition store. Their footsteps echoed as they made their way across the cavernous space, breaking the silence that had hung between them since Marek had announced their destination.

Marek seemed agitated as they reached a large machine. "Right. I suppose we'd better get going."

"Er…Marek?" Darren asked tentatively. "This bunker isn't your home, then?"

"Not where I grew up, no," Marek answered.

"What's the deal with your home?"

Marek didn't meet his eyes. "I don't want to talk about it." He checked all of his many suit pockets. "I'm all tech'd up…battery at ninety-three per cent charge. I think I'm ready."

Darren watched him. "What am I getting into?"

Marek paused and glanced at the silver tube-like machine. "Do you mean this device or the situation?"

"Both," Darren decided.

Marek patted the machine. "This is the Super SQUID. It has a far better range than the SQUID. It can transport us anywhere in Britain and a bit beyond, depending on weather conditions. I don't use it often. We just stand over here and it creates the interdimensional overlap around us." Marek walked into position as he explained.

Darren didn't follow him. "What about the situation?"

Marek pulled an angst-filled face. "Do you really need to know?"

"Yes."

"In case you hadn't noticed," Marek pointed out, "you do some of your best work when you have no idea what's going on."

Darren shook his head. "I'm kind of sick of that."

Marek rubbed his temples. "Miss Inghart infiltrated my life when I was growing up."

Darren's jaw dropped. "She knew you as a kid?"

"Yes," Marek answered, his face tight with tension. "When I ran away, I coded something of my own design called Concealable Latent Aggregation Malware, or CLAM for short, that I used to infect all the devices in the farmhouse. The CLAM aggregated the data from all of their devices, including their communications as they prepared to evacuate the site, in case I...er...took action against them. The problem is, I can only get the data from inside the farmhouse itself because of their network security controls. There's no way to exfiltrate the data without physical access. Getting inside has never been worth the risk before, but now we have no choice."

Darren breathed out slowly. "This is going to be dangerous, right?"

"Undoubtedly," Marek agreed as he put on his night-vision goggles and started up the Super SQUID. "Come on."

Miss Inghart paced the length of the warehouse while Dr Sanchez, Head of Surveillance, and his team watched a bank of screens that monitored the London area. The whole team looked tired after weeks of watching for a first move from Marek. Miss Inghart felt agitated despite her own fatigue. The echo of her heels clicked loudly over the quiet murmur of conversation. On the far side of the room, Ducas lay sleeping on a camp bed. Years of elite combat training in the Special Boat Service meant he was able to fall asleep in a heartbeat and wake up just as quickly, ready to fight.

It was a skill Miss Inghart envied.

Half of the team began to gather around a single screen. Dr Sanchez himself watched them, hawklike, until he was beckoned over. Miss Inghart waited, reminding herself that this could be another false alarm, and listened to the tone of the doctor's quiet questions asked in his distinctive West Coast American accent. His soft tone seemed at odds with the cut-throat reputation he had built while working for the CIA. He turned towards her and nodded.

Miss Inghart quickly walked over. "What do we have?"

He pointed at a map of Britain on the screen. "A big surge in electricity use in the London area followed by an increase in ultraion readings. Just like the last few times Marek has appeared. Judging by how far he got on his previous bigger energy surge, he's somewhere within this sixty-mile radius. Within that, there are three high-value targets of ours, plus the Farm."

"Good work!" Miss Inghart ran towards the warehouse doors. Ducas was already sitting in their BMW. She slid into the passenger seat, then pulled out her phone as Ducas drove off. "UK field teams are off black, repeat, off black! Command team is on the move. Teams Alpha, Beta, Gamma and Delta, secure your locations. Lethal force is authorized. Team Epsilon, proceed to the runway and await further orders with engines hot. Team Omega, secure known

London return points." She slid her phone into her pocket as they reached the main road, thick with evening traffic.

Ducas glanced at her as he joined the stream of cars. "You just put the whole of XSP's UK operational capability in the field. This had better work."

Miss Inghart didn't acknowledge his words. "Blues and twos, please, Mr Ducas."

Ducas pressed a button on the steering wheel. Sirens blasted into life and their flashing blue lights reflected off the silver paintwork of the car in front as it moved out of their way.

"Where to?" he asked.

"The Farm," Miss Inghart answered, watching for his reaction.

He gave a small, determined smile. "Home sweet home."

CHAPTER 15

THE FARM

Once Darren's eyes adjusted to the darkness outside, he realized they were standing in a copse of trees under a clear starry sky. He breathed in the cool air and felt himself relax as a breeze brushed his face.

Marek was checking his phone. "They know we're out. We don't have long."

"How?"

"Does it matter? It's what they've been waiting for."

"So what now?"

Marek adjusted his night-vision goggles and pointed south towards a farmhouse that stood some distance up a muddy track. "We need to get in there."

Darren thought for a moment. "Hop on."

Marek wrapped his arms around Darren's shoulders. Darren shinned up a smooth trunk and then jumped towards the tallest tree in the copse. Marek gave a nervous squeak as they sailed through the air, gripping tighter as Darren landed on a broad branch.

Darren climbed until the trunk began to creak under their combined weight.

"Get on that branch," he told Marek.

"Imagine for a moment that I have my eyes closed."

"Reach to your left."

Marek's left hand slowly released Darren and groped for the branch. The moment Marek took hold of it, Darren prised his right hand free and swung Marek at the branch.

Marek scrambled to get a grip with both hands. "I'm falling. I'm definitely falling!"

Darren put a hand under Marek's flailing foot and pushed him fully onto the branch, until Marek lay clamped to it using all four limbs. Darren climbed a metre higher and looked out at the farmhouse. It cut a dark, lonely figure at the edge of endless fields. Most of it seemed old, but it had a higgledy-piggledy feel to it – as though rooms had been added many times over a few hundred years. "Looks empty."

"It is."

"It's buzzing."

"You can hear that from here?"

"Yeah."

"It's a sonic sweeper alarm system. It detects movement in the grounds."

"Are those laser beams in the hedge?"

"Infrared beams. I wondered if you'd see those. There are other alarms as well. Here." Marek gingerly let go of the branch with one hand and passed Darren a visor. "Press the button behind your right ear."

Darren put the visor on and pressed the button. Bright flashes flickered on the farmhouse door and windowpanes. "What's that?"

"Ultraviolet detection system."

"Cool glasses."

"Thanks. They're stealth-enabled on the outside too. Oh, and they work as sunglasses."

Darren watched the Farm thoughtfully. There was a large oak overhanging the hedge near the gable end of the house. He estimated the distance from there to the roof. It wasn't an easy jump, but he knew he could do it.

"Any alarms on the roof?"

Marek smiled. "None."

"You okay if I smash a hole in the roof?"

"Be my guest."

Darren remained still, thinking. "I thought this would be harder."

"My thoughts exactly." Marek slipped and clumsily

stopped his fall by wedging one foot between two smaller branches.

Darren sighed. "You want to get down?"

"In as controlled a way as possible, yes!"

"Hop on again then."

Back on the ground, Darren waited for Marek to finish brushing tree debris from his suit. "It's a trap," he said.

Marek nodded. "Yes. It's too easy to get past those defences. In there will be something designed to kill me."

"So what's your Plan A?"

"You go in for me."

Darren frowned. "So I get killed for you?"

"Oh, I doubt that," Marek answered. "It takes very different things to kill the two of us."

"They'll use xenocide or something?"

"Maybe, but I'm sure they'll get as creative as their little brains can manage."

Darren shifted uneasily. "What if there's just a big bomb?"

Marek shrugged. "Darren, if you're blown into tiny pieces then I will indeed owe you a huge apology, but I doubt they'll use a bomb. I'm not saying they never blow things up, but they prefer to keep things quiet if they can. It comes with being so super-secret."

Darren mulled over Marek's words. "So maybe I get into the attic? What then?"

Marek handed him a small device. "Press the red button and drop it through the attic trapdoor. It'll beep a lot while it does its thing."

"What's it do?"

"They've put a disruption field up around the house. It stops me SQUIDing in or scanning the inside. This disrupts their disruptor."

"Anything else?" Darren asked.

"No."

Darren pulled up his hood, zipped up the neck to cover his nose and mouth, and switched on his stealth camo. "This won't run out of batteries, will it?"

Marek shook his head. "No. It charges using your movement."

Darren felt a shiver of adrenaline. "See you later then."

As he moved noiselessly up the track, Darren was amazed to find that his outfit didn't interfere at all with his movement or hearing. He felt part of the night, like a ghost under the stars. He grinned to himself and moved quicker. He made for the oak and scaled it until he was a few metres above the level of the slate roof. This close, the buzzing was almost deafening and, as he surveyed the area, his vision became blurry. Guessing it was the effect of the disruptor field, he pressed the button on his visor and relied on his own eyes.

Dew glistened on the roof as he judged his jump. He shifted his weight and felt the branch give slightly under him as he took off. He landed in a skid and began to slide down the tiles. With the edge approaching rapidly, he punched his hand through a slate and the waterproof lining beneath it. A ripping sound filled his ears as he came to a halt while slates slid over the edge, smashing on the ground. He lay there, catching his breath. Hearing nothing more but the constant buzzing, he hauled himself up and widened the gash in the roof until he could fit his head and shoulders through.

For a moment, he hung upside down and listened, then he dropped quietly onto a wooden ceiling joist. The attic wasn't what he'd expected. It was completely empty and strangely clean, as though the house had never been lived in. Air-conditioning pipes ran the length of the roof space. Darren put any curiosity aside, dropped down and crept silently towards the trapdoor. It wasn't designed to be opened from above, so he dug his nails into the wood and ripped out the hinges. The tearing sound filled the attic space, making him wince, but there was no response from below. He hung batlike once more, with his head and shoulders suspended in mid-air beneath the trapdoor hole. The house seemed deserted, the silence complete except for his breathing. Below him was what looked like a living room with two doors. One led to a landing, where from his vantage point he could see wooden stairs. The other door led directly to another room and seemed newer, as though the other room was an extension added at some later time. He activated Marek's device and dropped it down to the floor. Moments later, the buzzing stopped. Darren waited, still hanging. Minutes passed until a circle of swirling colours appeared. He smiled and dropped down as Marek exited the circle and switched off his SQUID.

Marek turned in a circle, taking in what Darren assumed must have been a familiar room.

"Well done," he said quietly and pulled out some kind of scanner from a pocket. He aimed it at each wall in turn and didn't look happy. "Nothing. No sensors. No electronic devices at all. Nothing even slightly like a trap."

"That's good, right?"

Marek shook his head. "It just means I'm missing something."

Smelling the musty odour of a deserted room, Darren brushed his hand across the wooden floor as Marek walked to the windowsill and picked up a photo frame.

"It's dusty," Darren said, looking at his hand. "No one's been here in ages."

"Two years, perhaps," Marek answered as he looked at the photo. "That's when I ran away." He stroked the picture with three gentle fingers. Darren looked at the photo. It showed a man and woman smiling happily and holding a baby. The thin, huge-eyed child could only be Marek. With surprise, Darren saw similarities between Marek and his parents. His mother's eyes were large, although far kinder than her son's. His father was waving with a very long-fingered hand. It seemed the features Darren had assumed were completely to do with Marek's alien heritage were not all they seemed.

Darren stayed crouching as he pondered this and clapped the dust from his hands. "They seem nice, your mum and dad."

"I don't remember them. They died when I was two years old." Marek pointed to a photo of a pleasant-looking old woman. "Grandma Masters brought me up at first. The last of my relatives to die." He replaced the photo he was holding and walked towards the doorway. "Let's look around."

Darren watched him as he passed, wondering what the complicated expression on his face meant. Marek's footsteps echoed across the room.

"STOP!"

Marek stopped and turned. "What is it?"

"The floorboard by the door. It's odd."

Marek rolled his eyes. "This is a two-hundred-year-old

farmhouse. All the floorboards are odd. They're all worn or warped or both."

"That one isn't," Darren answered as he stood and walked past Marek to inspect the board in question.

Marek crouched beside Darren. "You're right. It's been replaced."

Darren pointed. "The one on the other side of the door is the same."

"Darren, can you lift the board beside this one? Carefully, please."

Darren prised the worn floorboard away.

Marek rested his cheek against the floor so that he could see underneath the replacement floorboards that guarded the doorway. "There's some kind of pressure switch. I think you can take off the board above it, though."

Darren lifted the pristine floorboard away, exposing a long flat plastic panel with a metal contraption underneath. Marek pulled a penknife and screwdriver from a pocket and started to work on the contraption.

"It's entirely mechanical," he said as he worked. "My sensors only work on electricals. Clever!" He pushed his entire hand underneath and pulled out what looked like a clear glass aerosol can. "And here's the weapon."

"A bomb?"

"No, I don't think so." Marek held up the weapon and

pulled out a small torch from his pocket. Darren couldn't see a beam as Marek removed his goggles and shone it on the clear glass.

"It's a blacklight torch – it can shine an ultraviolet light beam as well as having a visible light setting," Marek explained. "I might be able to tell what the liquid is from the way it scatters the light, since I can see both kinds." He studied the weapon, the torch's beam alternating between visible and ultraviolet light. After a while, he laughed. "Oh, that is nasty!"

"What is it?"

Marek shook his head. "Strawberry juice!"

"What, is that all?"

"It's very clever, really. I'm highly allergic to strawberries, remember? This lets out a fine spray into the air, I breathe it in and I die in minutes. The brilliant thing is that if some local kid breaks in, it won't kill them. It's a weapon specifically made for me."

"Grim."

Marek handed Darren his xenodrenaline syringe as he replaced his goggles. "Just in case we set one off by mistake. Remember, you inject me in—"

"I remember." Darren accepted the syringe.

Marek disarmed an identical trap on the other side of the door and walked into a bedroom. Debris from tech experiments on the floor and a ceiling decorated to look like the night sky made it obvious that this had been Marek's room. Darren's attention was drawn to a large wall mirror. Something about it bothered him, but he wasn't sure what.

"This access point will do." Marek was kneeling by a phone socket on the wall by his bed. He removed the front, placed a small silver gadget onto the wire and turned to Darren. "Just let me access the network by linking to my phone..." Marek held his phone beside the gadget. "Phone, meet CLAM. CLAM, meet phone." He looked at Darren. "It'll take a few minutes to decompress the data and copy it to my phone. Then we can get out of here."

Darren nodded and looked around the room. One wall was devoted to old DVDs, stacked floor to ceiling. From the covers he recognized, they all seemed to be sci-fi movies. Another wall was covered in various scrawls and drawings on overlapping bits of paper, all held on with Blu Tack. He returned his attention to the mirror. He walked back into the lounge and he suddenly understood what was bothering him. The mirror on the lounge wall looked exactly the same and was hung exactly opposite its twin in Marek's bedroom. Darren ran a hand along the wall and tapped it. It sounded hollow.

"Marek?" he called.

"Shush, I'm working!"

"Okay," he muttered, and then punched the wall by the living-room mirror. The wall caved in easily. Darren smelled stale air escaping through the gap and used both hands to create a Darren-sized hole. He climbed through into the space between the two rooms and found himself standing in a narrow corridor with two-way mirrors to either side of him, set into the walls. Darren watched Marek through the bedroom mirror, sitting on his bed as he studied the data his phone was collecting, and felt a deep sense of unease at the idea that his companion had been spied on in exactly this way for years. He looked down the corridor and saw a vertical shaft with a ladder. He used it to descend to the ground floor and to his surprise saw that the shaft went through the floor into a basement. Darren continued down and found himself in a windowless room that seemed oddly modern for such an old house. Large lights were set into the walls and a piece of furniture that looked like a cross between a bed and a dentist's chair stood in the middle of the room. A few machines sat idle, a fine layer of dust on the screen of a medical-looking monitor. It took him a moment to work out what he was seeing and then a queasy sensation invaded his stomach.

He was standing in the middle of an operating theatre.

He turned and rapidly scaled his way back up the ladder. "Marek?" he called as he climbed out into the lounge.

Marek was standing at the lounge window with the photo of his parents in his hand. He didn't respond.

"Marek? You should see this," Darren said as he walked over. "You *need* to see this."

Marek still didn't respond, but just continued to look at the photo. Darren gripped his shoulder. "Marek?" he said again. And then another photo hanging on the wall caught his eye. It showed Marek at about six years old, smiling happily while sitting on the knee of a woman who was hugging him tightly. "Marek, is that…Miss Inghart?"

Marek slowly turned towards Darren, the photo of his parents gripped tightly in one hand and his phone in the other. His eyes drifted between his phone and the photo, his face locked in an expression of horror.

Darren shook Marek's shoulder. "Marek? Look at me. *Marek!*"

Marek flapped like a rag doll in Darren's hands, but didn't respond. Marek's eyes scanned the room as though he was seeing it for the first time.

"Marek!" Darren shouted, but then stopped. There was a new sound outside the building. A high-pitched *thwupp*ing noise. Darren looked out and saw a drone hovering at window height. A flap opened on the drone's underside and a missile descended into view. He grabbed Marek around the waist and dashed towards the hole in the wall. Behind him, he heard the window shatter just as he dived through, pulling Marek into the hidden corridor.

A huge explosion rocked the whole farmhouse. Marek seemed not to hear as Darren pushed him towards the ladder. Fire flooded the corridor as Darren slid down with Marek over his shoulder towards the relative safety of the basement.

He sat Marek down on the floor amongst the operating-theatre equipment as the house above started to groan. Then a second explosion made even the basement shake.

"Marek, do the SQUID. Marek!" Darren shouted as Marek looked about, confused at the sight of the operating theatre. "Marek? What's wrong? You're scaring me now. Marek? *MAREK!*"

Marek shook his head and whispered something to himself.

Darren held Marek's face with both hands as the temperature in the basement began to rise. "Look at me. Look at me!"

Hazy smoke began to fill the room and Marek suddenly sniffed. His eyes focused on Darren. "Fire."

"Yes, Marek, yes! Fire! SQUID us, quick!"

Marek pulled the SQUID out of his pocket and shone it at the far wall. The circle of light drifted left and right in Marek's shaking hand. Darren took the SQUID from him and Marek's hand fell limply to his side.

The ceiling creaked dangerously and chunks of plaster began to fall all around them. "Okay," Darren said, keeping his voice calm despite the intense heat radiating from the fire above. "You go through. I'll follow."

Marek looked at him, seemingly dazed and unaware of the danger around him. Finally he walked into the swirling colours. As soon as he was gone, Darren dived through and the ceiling collapsed behind him.

CHAPTER 16

THE FALLOUT

Miss Inghart picked her way through the mud towards the black van parked down the track from the fire engines that were fighting the blaze at the farmhouse. She climbed in the back to find Ducas standing with the Delta team commander. Behind them, the team's tech support leader was studying two wide screens.

"Commander Kahn."

"Ma'am."

"Report, please."

Commander Kahn glanced at Ducas and then began his report. "There was a disturbance on the farmhouse roof seven minutes after we received your order to come off black. Thermal imaging showed no life signs, but I assumed this was Marek Masters entering so I gave the order to close in to the edge of the property. Six minutes later, we saw movement in the bedroom. I deployed the heavy drone to carry out a rotation of the property and thermal imaging picked this up through the upstairs living-room window." He pointed to a screen that showed a thermal image of Marek standing in front of the window.

"He was the only one there?"

"Yes. We couldn't tell for sure what he was holding. Too big to be a phone."

"A photo frame," Miss Inghart said.

Commander Kahn continued. "The fact that Masters had moved between rooms indicated he'd disarmed the aerosol trap, so I gave the lethal force order. We deployed a double missile attack from the drone."

Miss Inghart's pulse quickened. "Tell me you got him."

Commander Kahn pointed at the screen again. "Watch."

Miss Inghart watched the recording as a target appeared, covering Marek's chest. The image began to close in on him as the missile flew towards the window. Then Marek seemed to partly disappear and fly backwards towards a hole in the far wall. A fraction of a second later, the missile exploded.

Miss Inghart looked at Ducas. "What was that?"

Ducas pointed to the tech leader, who answered nervously. "I've sent it to HQ for analysis. I can't be sure, but it seemed like some kind of stealth technology partly obscured Masters."

Commander Kahn continued. "We registered a peak in ultraion readings two minutes later. It looks like Masters escaped."

"Why didn't you use a xenocide dart?" Miss Inghart shouted. "There was no need to send the drone that close – that's why he heard it, and that's why he escaped! On top of that, now I have to try to make your missile explosion look like a gas leak!"

Commander Kahn glared at her.

Ducas stood between them. "Lads, can we have the van?"

Commander Kahn stalked out, scowling, followed by his tech lead.

Ducas shut the van door. "You should go easy on the commander. You might need a favour one day."

"He blew up the farmhouse!"

Ducas fixed her with a firm but sympathetic stare. "His op was good. He followed procedure."

"Right up to the point that he blew the place up and somehow missed Marek!"

"He followed a lethal force order. Your order. And he didn't miss Marek. Marek got out of the way."

"A xenocide dart from a sniper is all he had to do. No sound, no warning!"

Ducas shook his head. "The window would've stopped the dart. He could've used another sniper to shatter the window with a bullet first, but Marek was standing too close to the glass. The bullet would have knocked him down. The xenocide sniper would have had no clear view and we both know that if you put a bullet in Marek Masters, he doesn't stay dead."

"All right, all right!" Miss Inghart snapped and then breathed deeply. "Ifan, I've got nothing. You understand? This was the only move I knew Marek would make. God knows what sensitive information he found in that house, but if he got *anything* then he'll hurt us with it, and I can't even tell Mrs Lahaine or the General where, when or how that might happen. There's no coming back from this. I'll be out of XSP and you know what that means!"

Ducas watched her quietly. "Maybe the next move isn't Marek's."

Miss Inghart paused. "What do you mean?"

Ducas pointed at the screens. "That stealth-enabled thing that saved Marek. I bet you it was Devlin."

"Okay, but so what? Devlin is Marek's pawn."

Ducas grinned. "You sure about that? We know they split up in London for a while and we had that unconfirmed report that sounded a lot like Devlin and Marek arguing in a park."

"And that means what, exactly?" Miss Inghart asked impatiently.

"You can't play chess if your pawn won't do what it's told."

She began to follow Ducas's thinking. "So the question is…what's *Devlin's* next move?" She thought for a while and then pulled out her phone. "He'll do what people on the run always do in the end."

"What's that?"

Miss Inghart smiled. "Go home."

Darren staggered through the SQUID portal, holding Marek up with one arm. "Marek?" he said nervously. "We're back in the bunker."

Marek just stared at the floor and didn't reply. Not knowing what else to do, Darren helped him along to the Command and Control centre. He sat Marek at the table and waited. Marek remained motionless, holding the framed photo of his parents so tightly in his twin-thumbed grip that the protective glass cracked.

An eerie silence enveloped Darren as he stood there, feeling helpless. "Marek, you're scaring me."

Marek didn't answer, but finally seemed to become aware of his surroundings. He looked at Darren with a strange, inhuman expression on his face and whispered, "Lies."

Unsure how to deal with Marek's strange mood, Darren didn't answer.

Marek's expression hardened. "It's all lies," he said, and then devoted himself to his phone.

"Er, Marek? What was Miss Inghart doing in that picture?"

Marek gave a hollow laugh. "Nanny Inghart, you mean?"

Darren gaped. "She was your *nanny*?"

Marek looked up at him. "She looked after me when Granny Masters got too old. Then Granny died when I was six and Nanny fostered me – or at least that's what she claimed," he explained, a pained expression on his face.

"I don't understand," Darren answered. "I thought you said she infiltrated your life. You never said she brought you up!"

Marek didn't respond. Instead, he stood and watched the big central screen. Darren looked at the photographs now displayed there and understanding slowly dawned. One photo was identical to the framed shot of Marek's parents that he was still clutching. The others showed Marek's parents separately, but they seemed somehow different. The woman's eyes weren't as large and the man's fingers were not oddly long. Darren realized the truth: the photo Marek was holding had been altered to make the two people look more like Marek.

"I downloaded these photos from communications infiltrated by the CLAM." Marek turned from the screen and placed his free hand on the table. "I thought Nanny Inghart wormed her way into my life when I was six – a spy in Granny Masters's house. But no. It was *all* lies. All of it. The data I've found details their plan to fake my entire life. The house, the Farm, even Granny Masters. Project Helix made it all up and Miss Inghart was always there, in the shadows, from the very beginning. She hired Granny Masters to play my grandmother and designed the whole thing!" Pain filled his face as he looked at Darren. "Even the only picture I had of Mother and Father – they were just models adjusted to look a bit like me so that I wouldn't ask too many questions about my appearance… And what was that basement you took me down to? An operating theatre? I don't remember that at all. What did they do to me in there? I don't remember ever being sick, but I heal quickly. They could have operated on me and I would never know. I can't believe they tricked me for so long! I SHOULD HAVE SEEN THIS!"

Darren wanted to answer, but found he had nothing to say. Marek lapsed into silence, looking at the floor. Suddenly, he lifted the photo frame holding the fake picture of his parents and smashed it against the table.

"Lies! LIES!" he screamed repeatedly before throwing it at a screen. Robots scurried for cover as he picked up anything he could grab and threw it at them, screaming as he did so. Darren ducked and then grabbed Marek's arms, pinning them to his sides.

Marek struggled and kicked his legs. "I'll kill her! I'm going to kill them all!"

"Marek!"

"Let me go! Let me go!"

"Calm down!"

Marek continued to struggle, his legs flailing. "No, no! No!"

"I won't let you go till you stop!"

Marek suddenly went limp in Darren's arms. Darren let go, ready to grab Marek again, but Marek seemed to regain his composure.

"You're not going to kill anyone," Darren said. "You're going to stay calm and you're going to think."

Marek made a frustrated gesture with both arms. "Darren, I think in nine dimensions. I've had plenty of time to think. I know what I have to do. Every memory in my head for the first twelve years of my life is a lie. A lie Nanny Inghart created. Can you imagine that? Can you imagine your family turning out to be totally fake? To suddenly know nothing about who you are or where you came from?"

"No," Darren admitted.

Marek looked at him with triumphant intensity. "No,

I thought not. They treated me like I was stupid and fed me false information. I *hate* false information! So, do you know what I'm going to do? I'm going to go through everything I've learned about the organization we're fighting to make sure I know what is really true and what's fake. Then I am going to destroy everything they know and everything they love. Then I will find dear Nanny Inghart and—"

Darren interrupted. "No killing, Marek. We agreed!"

Marek smiled coldly. "That deal's off."

There was a dreadful certainty in Marek's expression that unsettled Darren. He had no doubt that Marek was serious about the threats he was making.

"Then I walk," Darren answered.

Marek's lips grew thin. "Oh, and where would you go?"

"Home," Darren said firmly, and then felt uncertain. "Maybe."

Marek snorted. "And how will you do that? You can't even read a map or a train timetable! You'll never survive without me."

Darren stepped back as though he'd been slapped. "I'll find a way," he said and turned to walk away.

"Really?" Marek sneered in mocking disbelief.

Darren paused at the door, anger bubbling inside at how Marek had used his reading problems against him. "I've been stupid for my whole life. I'll survive."

"Have it your way!" Marek shouted as Darren lolloped away, mini-SQUID in hand.

Miss Inghart woke up to find Ducas's hand over her mouth. With his free hand he put a finger to his lips and then mouthed the word *window*. He padded silently to the apartment door and left. Leaving the lights off, Miss Inghart crept to the window and looked out at the alley below. The familiar figures of the General and Mrs Lahaine stood in silence. Mrs Lahaine's shoulders were hunched against the cold of the night. Miss Inghart quickly grabbed a remote listening device and pointed it at the pair in the alley.

Ducas appeared after about a minute. "Sir. Ma'am."

"At ease."

Ducas relaxed his pose in response to the General's order.

"Where is she?" Mrs Lahaine asked.

"Asleep," Miss Inghart heard Ducas lie.

The General spoke in a loud whisper, as though he had been holding in his wrath for hours. "Chaos. Total chaos! We go dark for five weeks and what do we get? A set of muddy footprints and a house fire we can't explain! Does she know how much that dark period cost us? Does she know how much effort we are having to put in to cover our tracks?"

"She accepts full responsibility," Ducas answered calmly.

"I bet she does!" the General answered in a whispered bark.

Mrs Lahaine spoke icily. "Her recommendation that we alter our focus to capture or kill Darren Devlin as a way of drawing out Marek Masters is denied. The Council will issue a kill order on Miss Inghart."

In the room above, Miss Inghart was gripped by a wild, absurd desire to run, even though she knew with Ducas on her tail she wouldn't survive till dawn.

"They haven't issued the order yet?" Ducas asked.

"It's just a matter of time," Mrs Lahaine answered. "She's had chances… I gave her chances. Most aren't that lucky."

Ducas thought for a moment. "Sir, ma'am, it is Devlin's sister's birthday in two days' time. He won't miss it."

The General sounded surprised. "Can you be sure of that?"

Ducas shrugged. "Miss Inghart interviewed him. Devlin and his sister have a very strong bond. Daisy Devlin has always been his protector. His anchor, you know? He will return. That's what Inghart said."

Miss Inghart held her breath, waiting to see if Ducas could persuade them.

"In for a penny, sir," Ducas continued. "We've come this

far. We might as well have one last crack at stopping this getting out of control. My mission, not hers. If Marek is alive in three days' time, I'll take out Miss Inghart, but I could do with her knowledge of Masters and Devlin for this op."

The General glanced at Mrs Lahaine and they began a whispered conversation that Miss Inghart couldn't hear. Eventually, the General addressed Ducas. "You've seen the boy's home. What is your tactical assessment?"

Relief flooded through Miss Inghart.

"It's a difficult location," Ducas answered. "Devlin is very cautious and seems to be tactically aware as well as exceptional at hiding. It would take a double team to secure the surrounding streets, but he would spot that level of presence."

"You're making it sound impossible," the General pointed out.

"No, just hard," Ducas answered. "There's an acre of woods behind the house. He will access the house by that route."

"How do you know?" Mrs Lahaine asked.

"Because that's what I'd do," Ducas answered. "In the woods he'll spot anything out of place more easily. He'll probably know it well. We can hide two operatives at most. They have to be top-class snipers, ambush experts and close-combat specialists."

"That's a rare mix." The General smiled humourlessly. "Other than you, Mr Ducas, do we have anyone up to the task?"

Ducas tipped his head as he considered his answer. "Up to my standards? No. Not that I've seen. Not who's still alive, anyway."

The General didn't answer at once. "Then we deploy the XCEL."

"XCEL? What's that?" Ducas asked.

Mrs Lahaine answered. "It's beyond top secret." She turned to the General. "It uses technology that we've still not been able to replicate. We'll need Council approval."

"I'll see to it," the General answered. He looked at Ducas. "Return to the safe house. You'll receive the official order in the morning."

"Yes, sir."

Miss Inghart retreated into the room and waited for Ducas to return.

"You heard?" he asked when he entered.

She placed a hand over her heart. "Thank you."

Ducas shook his head. "You don't have long to prove yourself. If they end up issuing a kill order on you, I'll make sure I get the mission – that way, you can at least get a head start. But you'd better hope Devlin turns up."

"I know. He will." She stepped towards him and whispered,

"Listen, if the XCEL attacks Devlin, you mustn't join in. It won't hesitate to injure or even kill you if you get in the way."

Ducas looked wary. "Are you going to tell me what it is?"

Miss Inghart sat on the bed and thought of how to begin. She knew her face must look haunted. "It's how this ends."

CHAPTER 17

THE KINDNESS OF STRANGERS

Darren spent the day hidden under his arch behind St Pancras station, letting the events at the Farm and afterwards sort themselves out in his head. His emotions bounced between humiliation and anger as he remembered Marek taunting him about not being able to read, but beneath all that he felt confused and betrayed by what Marek had kept secret from him. He couldn't understand how Marek could hate lies and yet hide how well he had known Miss Inghart – that he'd actually been brought up by her. The only explanation he could think of was that Marek really thought he was too stupid to understand. After all Marek's praise of Darren's abilities, that hurt the most.

He felt ready to lash out, but a far more powerful feeling began seeping through his anger and disbelief until it overwhelmed every thought in his head: a nervousness that kept his mind coming back to his mum and dad and especially to Daisy. He couldn't stop wondering how strange it would be to discover one day that the people who linked you to the world through every memory in your head did not even exist.

Eventually, his anxiety morphed into an energy that forced him to stand and leave his hiding place. He was gripped by a need to see his family and reassure himself that they were okay after all these weeks away.

"Hey, Darren!" Robbie, Grant and Devina were walking into view, apparently at the end of a long shift. They beckoned Darren over.

"Where've you been, kid?" Robbie tipped his head. "You got a new outfit."

Darren glanced down at his camo jacket and for the first time felt uncomfortable wearing the gift from Marek. "Orange didn't suit me."

"Ha!" Grant laughed, but then his smile faded. "You all right, son?"

Darren plunged his hands deep into his pockets. "Been better. Missing home."

"Where's home?"

"Farlington."

Robbie frowned. "Where?"

"Near Peterborough."

"Oh yeah, I think I know where you mean."

Devina smiled with relief. "Do you want us to call someone? They could come pick you up."

"No!" Darren said quickly. Fear rose in his chest at the idea of Miss Inghart finding him again.

Robbie raised a pacifying hand. "No one's calling anyone, okay?" He gave Devina a sharp look.

Darren relaxed. "Okay. I just want to see my sister. It's her birthday tomorrow, I think – is it the third?"

"Yes, it is..." Robbie raised an eyebrow towards Devina and Grant. "A word?"

The three walked away a short distance and began to whisper. Darren tuned into their conversation.

Devina shook her head. "Okay, Robbie. I don't like that look on your face."

"All I'm thinking is that I have to take the van to Stamford one day this week. So I could do it tomorrow. It's easy enough to go past Peterborough…"

Devina sucked her teeth in disapproval. "And then what?"

"He says he wants to see his sister. That might mean seeing his parents. Maybe he'll go home?"

Devina's tone was stern. "Robbie, my friend, just look at Darren. When he was all muddy, he could've been anyone. Now it's pretty clear he really is that boy who's been all over the news!"

"So? He's a nice kid. Nothing like what they're saying on the news. Something must be wrong with what's being reported."

"What do you mean, 'so'? Helping him is a criminal offence! You know what they said happened at the hospital and his school."

Robbie sighed. "Devina, come on! How does a twelve-year-old destroy a school? We can't bring him in, you must know that. He's got a family, right? He wants to see them. Whatever is really going on, they'll be the best people to help him. Trust me, that's his way out of this."

Devina snorted.

"Worth a try?" Robbie smiled imploringly. "Come on, we can help him make a good choice. Okay?"

Devina looked at Darren and then poked Robbie in the chest. "No! This is getting out of hand!"

Grant got between the two of them. "Easy, you two!"

Robbie held his ground. "I'm taking him!"

Devina stood and stared for a moment, clearly shocked. Then she turned and walked away, calling back, "On your own head be it, Robbie. I'm having nothing more to do with this!"

Robbie watched her go and then looked at Grant. "Well?"

Grant shifted uncomfortably. "I'll look the other way, mate, but that's all."

* * *

Twelve hours later, Darren sat hidden, surrounded by equipment in the back of a small van, while Robbie drove away from King's Cross and began to weave through busy London traffic. Darren tried to control his nervousness and slowly became lost in his thoughts. Today was Daisy's birthday. He wondered what kind of day she was having without him. He hoped she was as happy as she had been on every one of her birthdays that he could remember, but he feared she wasn't. She only ever seemed truly happy when all the family were too and especially him. His resolve hardened. He didn't just need to see her for himself, he needed to make her happy.

He was stiff from sitting amongst the assorted equipment by the time Robbie called back, "Almost at Peterborough. Climb over, Darren!"

Darren climbed into the front passenger seat. "How far?"

"Twenty minutes, maybe."

Darren looked out of the window. The countryside seemed familiar. "You didn't take the motorway?"

"Roadworks," Robbie explained. "You know I can only take you as far as Peterborough, right? Work check how far we drive."

Darren watched Robbie's tense expression and felt bad. He didn't feel like he deserved Robbie's help.

"Sorry about Devina."

Robbie forced a grin. "Don't you worry about her."

Darren watched him for a while in silence. "Will you get in trouble?"

"Don't worry about it," Robbie repeated firmly.

"Will they sack you?"

Robbie glanced at him before returning his eyes to the road. "Only if they catch me."

Darren looked guiltily at the dashboard.

Robbie seemed to read his mind. "So, when I was fifteen my parents split up. I went off the rails a bit. A lot, actually. Did some stupid things, you know? Ended up in big trouble. Then this woman helped me out. She didn't know me very well and she didn't have to help me, but she did. I got straightened out and, well, here I am. And now I'm helping you."

"Still, it's not…"

"Look, one day, someone will need help and you'll be able to help them," Robbie said. "That's how you make things right, okay?"

Darren smiled. "Nice idea."

Robbie nodded. "Yeah, it is… Promise me you'll help people whenever you can."

"I promise."

"Good lad."

Darren sat back and let the idea swirl in his mind. Minutes later, he saw a church spire in the distance and his heart jolted in his chest. He remembered visiting the church on a school trip and how it stood on the bank of the same river that, downstream, flowed past the back of his house.

"I know where I am!"

Robbie glanced at him. "You sure?"

"Yup! Let me out. I can go on my own."

Robbie pulled into a lay-by opposite a wheat field. They got out and Darren breathed in deeply. The countryside sounded comfortingly familiar after the din of London and the strange quietness of the bunker. He grinned.

Robbie wasn't smiling. "Are you sure you're going to be okay if I leave you in the middle of nowhere?"

Darren's grin broadened. "This isn't nowhere." He crossed the road and looked back. "Thank you!"

"Good luck!" Robbie called and waved.

Darren waved back and then vaulted the hedge. He lolloped north-west, keeping the church to his right and weaving through rows of wheat stubble. He eventually reached the river and followed its course, seeing it change from a broad, lazy flow of water to narrower rapids as the ground dipped towards Farlington. Before it got too dangerous, he swam across and lolloped another twenty minutes until Farlington itself came into view. Then he lay hidden as he waited for the sun to set. Far ahead of him were the woods where he had spent so many evening hours hidden in the trees. Their gentle movements in the wind had been a constant soundtrack to the time he had spent trying to work out why he was so different. He smiled to himself, remembering the occasions when he had helped Daisy into the trees so that she could explain all the rules that everybody else seemed to understand.

Home stood behind those trees: the gateway between his wooded haven and the normal world outside. A halfway house where he was understood, but where normal-world rules still wrapped themselves around everything, making him feel bad for how he let his parents down. Especially Dad, who seemed to so keenly feel "other people's expectations".

The sun lowered, becoming a crown of flame, magnifying the reds and golds of the leaves still to fall from the trees. Activating his camo, he crept forwards. He paused to listen every few paces until he reached the treeline and then climbed. He took it slower than usual, ensuring he was silent, until he reached the higher branches and waited. The leaves rustled as the breeze changed direction, calling in the night, and he let the dark of the woods envelop him in their familiar embrace.

The woodland was only about a hundred metres deep, but it took Darren two hours to silently cross from tree to tree until he was in his favourite sycamore just metres from his garden fence. He settled onto a solid branch and watched the windows, guessing that the after-dinner routine was under way. The curtains were not yet closed, allowing yellow light to spill out and him to see in. He shifted along until he could see the dining room through the patio doors. Inside was a banner and a large balloon and, beyond that, the remains of a birthday meal on the table. He didn't need to see it to know that it was lasagne and chocolate cake. Daisy had asked for the same on every birthday he could remember.

Then she was there. She walked to the window and placed a palm on the glass. Darren raised his hand in response, but she didn't see him. Her gaze seemed far away. He wanted to speak, but the lump in his throat wouldn't let him. Then she vanished behind drawn curtains.

Darren sat in the darkness and wondered what to do. The strange grief that had gripped him at losing sight of Daisy gave way to a now familiar sense of uncertainty. He wanted, more than anything, to knock on the window and be drawn into his home by his family's welcoming arms. To hear the inevitable relief that would be in all their voices, even his dad's. But then what? What would his parents do?

They had let him go once, after all, and what if Miss Inghart or Mr Ducas came knocking now? What would happen to his family if he was found here?

With a sense of deepening guilt, he began to realize how stupid it was to have come home and how much danger he could put his family in. He stood to leave, but then the back door opened and Daisy stood silhouetted in the doorway, her shadow stretching towards him. He froze as she walked out and made her way to the fence. She stopped at the exact spot where she always waited for him to help her over. Torn, he watched her, desperate to call out, but knowing he mustn't. He knew he had to leave and lollop far from here to keep her safe. He stayed silent as he waited for her to retreat to the warm familiarity of the house, but she stayed for minute after minute and then began to cry. Huge tears rolled down her cheeks. Her shoulders shuddered with each sob, and any thought in Darren's mind of leaving was swept aside.

"Hey, Daisy," he called in a loud whisper.

She looked up, uncertain. "Tiny?"

He switched off his camo. "Yup."

Her face broke into a huge smile. "You came! Help me up, quick!"

CHAPTER 18

HOMECOMING

Daisy grabbed hold of Darren's neck and he clambered up to a familiar branch. He waited for Daisy to let go, but she didn't. She kept holding him tight. He shifted around and hugged her back.

"Happy birthday," he muttered into her shoulder.

"Thanks, Tiny," she said as she finally broke away and wiped tears from her eyes.

"I didn't get you a present."

She slapped him playfully. "Well, go get one then!"

Darren snapped off a twig and handed it to her with a grin. "It's the thought that counts."

Daisy laughed and finished wiping her eyes before taking it. "Better than last year's."

Darren shrugged. "You really needed new socks."

"I'm wearing them now! I still can't imagine how you

decided on the daisy-patterned ones." She smiled. "So good to see you!"

"Yeah, you too."

"Are you doing okay?"

Darren shrugged. "Kind of, I guess."

Daisy's eyes grew large. "Darren, I'm so sorry! If I hadn't persuaded you to go to school that day, none of this would've happened!"

Darren shook his head. "No. That's on me."

"No, Darren," Daisy answered. "They were bullying you. I could've stopped them."

"No." Darren put a hand on her shoulder. "I flipped out. I can't do that. I'm too strong."

"It's not your fault you're so strong! I mean, did you even know you could demolish walls?"

"Daisy," Darren said firmly. "It was my fault."

She seemed ready to continue arguing, but then stopped herself. A wicked gleam appeared in her eye. "Mind you, you did give Alex Harrison a lamp-post wedgie. You're officially forgiven for that!"

Darren laughed despite himself. "Okay. I'll take that!"

Daisy's face suddenly grew serious. "Are you okay, really?"

Darren shrugged. "It's hard being away, you know?"

"It's hard you being away," Daisy admitted. "I mean…

I'm back at school and Mum and Dad are trying to go back to work, but I can tell we're all worrying about you all the time. Dad gets snappy and then Mum cries."

"I'm sorry."

Daisy grabbed his arm and said urgently, "But it's not safe to come back! The police have the street under surveillance and that Dr Wiseman keeps ringing. She keeps persuading Mum and Dad to stay put and not try to find you. She isn't what she says she is."

"Yeah, I know," Darren answered. "The guy who broke me out of prison told me all about her."

"Is that the other boy on the news?"

"Marek, yeah."

Daisy shifted uneasily. "He sounds like trouble."

"Yeah, he is," Darren admitted.

Daisy's tone became disapproving. "I don't like the sound of that."

Darren smiled reassuringly. "I think we're done with each other. He was okay most of the time, but he just—"

"Just what?"

Darren wondered how to explain Marek Masters. It was hard to know where to start. "He thinks faster than he feels. He can do some pretty bad things when he's not feeling."

Daisy pulled a face. "Sounds like a psycho."

Darren tipped his head. "That's what Dr Wiseman said. That's not her real name. Thanks for that warning you sent."

She smiled. "It helped?"

"Stopped me getting caught. She's a spy or something. Her real name is Inghart."

Daisy sighed. "At least I got something right. I heard her on the phone discussing moving you to Bleakmoor. She said something about a chemical tracker in your food. It just sounded really dodgy. Then she came back and she was saying we should all record messages for you and it just... well, it didn't feel right when she was going on about you being too dangerous to go near..." She tailed off and then looked at him more closely as the light from a rising full moon grew brighter. "Hey, what's with the outfit?"

"You like it?" Darren asked, realizing that he cared more about her answer than he'd expected.

"Yes, wow! Where's my scruffy brother gone? You almost look cool! Is that a vintage punk T-shirt?"

"I think so. What does it say?"

"*Pretty Vacant.*"

Darren smiled. "Brilliant!"

They fell silent for a moment and Daisy's worried expression returned. "What are you going to do now?"

"Dunno," Darren admitted. "Turns out I'm quite good at roughing it."

"Is there nowhere you can go though? Being out on the streets is really dangerous, you know."

Darren shook his head. "I don't know who to trust. Miss Inghart brought half the London police down on me just like that." He snapped his fingers. "Thing is…"

"What?"

"She's working for an organization. They've done some really bad stuff and they're everywhere. All over the world, maybe. Me and Marek, they did things to us and some other kids. I'm going to have to hide for ever or they'll kill me."

Daisy watched him, processing what he'd said. "What did they do?"

"Experiments." Darren couldn't work out how to explain what he had discovered about what he really was. It seemed too much to admit even to Daisy. "They tried to make some kids cleverer and stronger. Proper dodgy DNA stuff. Some kids died."

Daisy covered her mouth. "Oh my… Someone has to stop them!"

"Yeah, but it's only Marek who's trying and he wants to kill them all. That's why I walked out on him. I mean, I guess they need stopping and arresting or something, but he just goes way too far." Darren paused, a strange feeling gripping him as a thought he couldn't describe formed in his mind.

Daisy looked at him as though she was reading his mind. "You can't take this on alone, Darren," she said firmly.

Darren stared at the moonlit branch. He tried to think of how to explain that although sometimes he felt twelve years old and totally lost, when enemies surrounded him, he had completely different instincts. He wondered how quickly monsters aged. Were they like dogs? Was part of him several times his human age? Several times more capable than the boy Daisy saw sitting in front of her? He didn't know how to explain any of that. He didn't even know if he was ready to.

He looked back at Daisy. "What if it's got to be me?"

"Do you really believe that, Tiny?"

Darren felt the heavy weight of truth in his answer. "I know it."

A ripple of sadness passed across Daisy's face, and then she gripped his shoulder. "Then it's like what Grandad used to say. You simply think, *What's right is right*, and just take it from there."

Darren felt a strange sense of resolve building inside him. "Thanks, Daisy."

She started to say something, but then frowned. "What's wrong?"

The hairs on the back of Darren's neck had started prickling as his monstrous instincts suddenly made him aware of something unseen – something watching them from the trees.

He grabbed Daisy around her waist and jumped, covering her mouth to stop her screaming, and landed in their garden. "GET IN THE HOUSE!" he roared. Then he turned, activating his camo as he searched the woods for movement.

"Darren, what is it?" Daisy asked, panic in her voice.

"RUN! INSIDE, NOW!"

CHAPTER 19

HIDING IN THE TREES

Daisy started to run and Darren was gripped with a need to keep whatever it was up there away from her. High to his left, he spotted two pinpricks of green light unlike anything he'd seen in the woods before. He jumped back over the fence and landed on a pine tree, climbing as high as it could take him. Then he saw it through the trees.

He thought it was a man dressed in a grey jumpsuit until it moved with the ease of a chimpanzee, gripping with its feet as well as its hands as it climbed, and then paused to look around itself with eyes that shone bright green from an otherwise featureless face. Suddenly it moved in a blur, so fast that Darren only had an instinctive sense of where it was by the sound and swaying of the trees as it slipped through them towards him. Darren found himself jumping backwards, relying on memory to know where there was a branch to land on.

With one last leap it was on him. As it raised a hand to strike, its skin turned a luminescent green, and for a moment it seemed as though Darren could see right through its human features to a metallic skeleton within. He saw a razor-thin arc of green light slash the air as it brought its arm down on him before he could dodge away, and he felt a stinging pain in his left wrist.

Growling, he swung under his perch and dropped straight down, branches slashing at his face, before pushing off the trunk to launch himself towards an ash tree. He felt the creature following him through the air, so he leaped off the ash and lashed out with a kick. He heard a satisfying thud as his foot hit the thing square in the chest, but it landed neatly on a nearby branch, apparently unharmed. Its face was entirely emotionless as its eyes shone across him; the skin of its bald head had a metallic greenish tint, matched by its grey-green jumpsuit. Then its eyes flashed brighter green and it was a blur once more, shooting towards him.

Another arc of green light. Darren felt a stinging pain in his shoulder as a smouldering branch fell past him. Guessing his attacker was using some kind of laser, he climbed high and jumped again. Behind him, his pursuer threw something. Branches all around him were sliced from trees and fell smoking to the ground below, as a storm of spinning laser-green stars flew past him. He felt some strike him and quietly thanked Marek for the protection his bullet-deflecting camo suit gave him.

He leaped again, aiming for a young pine, as a plan formed in his mind. He grabbed the tree high up and allowed his speed and weight to bend the whole trunk. Then, as the creature followed, making a blurred jump towards him, he let go and dropped to a thick sycamore branch. The pine whipped through the air and hit the thing in the face with enough force to knock a normal person out, sending it crashing through the canopy and thudding into the ground below. Darren breathed a sigh of relief and rubbed his shoulder, which stung from a deep cut – his bendy body armour not perfect enough to deal with a direct laser strike. He wondered how he'd ever get treatment without the police coming down on him. He thought, ruefully, that Marek would have known what to do.

Before he could react, a greenish-grey hand grabbed his ankle. He growled and kicked, but with no effect as the creature pulled him free of his branch and swung him at the tree trunk. Darren smashed into it and was winded immediately, then fell to the woodland floor. His head foggy, he staggered to his feet and lolloped towards the open ground beyond the woods and the river in the distance. Maybe he could outrun it.

He sensed it coming after him and started to zigzag through the trees as another storm of throwing stars slashed through the greenery around him. But he wasn't quick enough. A heavy punch landed between his shoulder blades, sending him sprawling into the leaf litter. He slid to a halt just short of open ground.

He turned over to see the thing balancing in perfect stillness in the lower branches of a giant oak, legs folded tight, ready to launch itself towards him. It drew back a fist and extended its fingers. Green light appeared under each of its nails and extended out into laser-claws. Darren held his breath, sensing with a dreadful certainty that he was about to die, and resolved that he wouldn't give it the satisfaction of a scream. *At least Daisy's safe in the house*, he thought to himself as the thing dipped its shoulders and in slow motion – or so it felt to Darren – began its leap.

Then suddenly something strange was happening. The oak swayed and rose from the ground as a huge, growing bubble engulfed the bottom of the tree. His pursuer looked down and began to climb rapidly to avoid the bubble as it spread. Giant roots ripped clear of the ground and Darren scrambled backwards as earth rained down on him. He watched in awe as the creature reached the top and the entire tree rose into the air. The great old oak tipped forward and began to spin, sending down a shower of leaves…and then it exploded, sending a shock wave of broken wood outwards, flattening Darren to the ground and deafening him. The strange creature was flung against a tree trunk and slid motionless to the ground.

Darren let out a breath of stunned relief, hardly able to process what he had just seen. It all seemed so unreal that he felt dizzy. Then, shockingly, he saw the creature rise, hardly damaged by the explosion, and climb nimbly back into the trees and out of sight. His eyes searched for it in the darkness, a sense of panic gripping him at not knowing where it was.

Then a shadow blocked the moonlight.

Darren turned to see someone tall and thin standing over him. His mind struggled to catch up with what he was seeing.

Marek held out a hand. "Come on! We've got to SQUID out of here, NOW!"

CHAPTER 20

21% MONSTER

"You came after me!" Darren gasped as he let Marek grab both his hands and try to heave him to his feet. The third attempt ended with Marek himself falling over from the effort.

Marek batted Darren's words away as he got up. "Of course I did! I just had to...never mind. Now, come on. We have to go!"

Darren rolled to his knees and stood. He looked up at the trees. "I don't see it."

Marek grabbed his shoulder and forced Darren to look at him. "It'll be watching us. Learning more before it attacks again. It won't be fooled by another QUIET bomb. It never gets fooled twice and, anyway, I've only got one left. Come on, we don't have much time!"

Darren followed Marek, who was fiddling with the

SQUID as he ran away from the trees. "I don't understand how it's still alive. What was that thing?"

Marek turned towards him, his insect-like night-vision goggles multiplying the desperate look of fear in his eyes. "An XCEL."

"X-what?"

"A Xeno-Cybernetically Enhanced Life-form," Marek answered. "A part-living and part-robotic being. A cyborg with genetically engineered human biology and alien technology."

Darren's jaw dropped. "That thing's part-human?" he asked as he continued nervously scanning the trees.

"No, not really." Marek fiddled nervously with the SQUID and almost dropped it. "Come on, stupid thing!" He glanced at Darren. "Keep an eye out for it. I can't believe they managed to make one! The hamster was one thing, but a human? It's lethal, Darren. Utterly lethal."

As fear gripped him again, Darren's sensitive ears picked up the faint sound of something cutting through the air. Instinctively, he dived towards Marek and knocked him down. A black dart thudded into a tree above their heads. Darren picked up Marek and lolloped towards the river. Another dart fizzed towards them, making Darren dive and drag Marek towards a small boulder that lay in the long grass near the Old River Road. He slid them in behind it as a third dart skimmed past, only centimetres from them.

"My SQUID!" Marek yelled. "You idiot, you broke my SQUID!"

"Darts."

"What?"

"Someone's shooting at us."

"An XCEL wouldn't shoot darts."

"Shush."

"Of course—"

"Shhh!"

Marek finally fell silent, allowing Darren to listen. "It's Ducas," he whispered.

"How do you know?" Marek asked quietly.

"I remember how he breathes."

"How he *breathes*? Only you, Darren. Where is he?"

"Behind us and moving slowly to our right along the treeline. He'll get a clear shot soon."

"We could move around too?"

"The boulder's the wrong shape. He'll still get the shot," Darren answered.

"Oh. Okay, give me your mini-SQUID."

Darren fished in his pocket and handed it over.

Marek inspected it with shaking fingers. "The battery is almost flat!"

"I've used it twice," Darren reminded him.

Marek muttered under his breath and then whispered, "I'm going to have to recode this since I locked it down pretty tightly. Then I need to hook it to my phone battery."

Darren listened to Ducas's slow and careful movements. "How long do you need?"

"Five minutes?"

"We've got two."

"Then we're dead!" Marek hissed as he continued reprogramming the mini-SQUID.

Darren thought about what to do. Part of him just wanted to lie there and rest. His wrist stung, his shoulder stabbed with pain and his back ached from his fight with the XCEL, but he pushed the pain down and forced himself to concentrate. "All right," he whispered. "I'm going to sneak up on Ducas and whack him before he can shoot us."

"Ducas?" Marek whispered. "You're going to sneak up on a special-forces sniper who's trained to kill with his bare hands...and thump him?"

"Yup."

"Are you mad?"

"I'm not mad," Darren answered quietly as he began to sneak out into the long grass. "I'm twenty-one per cent monster."

No dart came speeding through the air as he crawled away from the cover of the boulder. The camo really did its job. He lay still for a few seconds, listening hard. Ducas had stopped as well. Darren took a slow, deep breath and then held it. He focused his mind and allowed himself to dissolve into the world, his ears trained only on Ducas. As the sniper moved, Darren crawled on, metre by metre, to close the gap. Deep in his quietened mind, he wondered if this was how his monstrous ancestors had hunted – silent predators hidden in the dark of night, tracking unsuspecting prey. Then he reminded himself that it was a lethal assassin he was hunting, not some wild animal.

Ducas's careful, shallow breathing grew slowly louder as Darren approached. Still holding his own breath, he spotted the last centimetre of the underside of a gun barrel covered in camouflage. The barrel adjusted a fraction to the left as Ducas aimed at Marek, still lying beside the boulder. The man let out a slow breath, growing still as he got ready to fire.

Darren exploded out of his hiding place, grabbed the gun barrel and rammed the rifle butt into Ducas's face. Ducas yelled and rolled without letting go of the rifle. They struggled as Ducas gained his feet and Darren pushed into him, forcing the rifle barrel upwards – he heard it groan as it twisted in his hands. Suddenly Ducas spun, throwing Darren to the floor. Darren got to his knees just in time to block Ducas as the man brought the butt of the bent gun down like a club. Darren punched out hard at his chest, making Ducas stagger, and then grabbed Ducas's arms, ripping his hands from the twisted gun. They struggled until Darren landed a headbutt.

Ducas grunted with pain and broke away. Darren lunged, hoping to press his advantage, but realized too late that Ducas was exaggerating how badly he was hurt. He punched Darren in the throat and then spun to kick him in the stomach. Darren bellowed and moved backwards, staying out of range as the pain from his fight with the XCEL burned afresh. Every instinct was telling him to lollop away to give himself time to recover, but he knew he had to keep Ducas far from Marek. He growled and ducked under a punch and launched himself at Ducas. The man staggered backwards. Darren attacked again, but this time Ducas was ready – he sidestepped and tripped Darren who hit the floor hard and instantly lifted an arm to defend himself... but this time Ducas hung back.

He looked at Darren warily. "Kid, I don't want to hurt you. I only want Marek."

Darren slowly got to his feet, breathing hard. His wounds ached and he could feel himself getting tired in a way he never usually did.

Ducas settled into a karate-style pose. He watched Darren, blood flowing from his nose. "Come on, kid. I heard you talking to your sister. You care about people.

You know how that feels. You must know Marek doesn't care about you."

Darren studied him carefully, using the time to regain his breath. "You don't either."

"No, I don't," Ducas admitted. "But Marek's expecting you to die for him. That thing in the trees…if I don't get you, it will. Come on, give me Marek. I'll help you kill that thing if you do. Help you keep your sister safe."

Darren scanned Ducas's face, gauging whether he was lying. He couldn't tell either way. He decided to keep him talking. "You're why she's in danger."

"No," Ducas answered. "Give me Marek. You understand? Come on, kid. Marek isn't loyal. He'd kill you in a heartbeat if it suited him. He doesn't know how to care about anybody. He's a monster."

"How very kind of you to say so, Mr Ducas." Marek stood to Darren's right, smiling arrogantly.

"No!" Darren shouted as Ducas immediately leaped at Marek, who dropped to the ground and curled himself into a ball. Darren dived forwards, trying to grab Ducas's foot, but missed as Ducas lifted both fists high above his head and yelled a war cry like an avenging demon. Darren closed his eyes, anticipating the moment Ducas's blow smashed into Marek, but there was silence. When he opened them again, Ducas was nowhere to be seen.

Marek still lay curled up. Just above him, like a strange umbrella, was a disc of swirling colours. Marek looked up carefully and then switched off the mini-SQUID.

Darren helped him to his feet. "Nice move. Where'd you send him?"

Marek brushed mud from his suit. "The local sewage works. Now, let's get—"

Marek never finished the sentence. A look of intense fear gripped his face as he looked over Darren's shoulder. The hair on Darren's neck stood on end and he turned, knowing that he would see the XCEL, but what he saw still shocked him.

Being dragged by the XCEL, with her hair held tight in its grip, was Daisy.

Darren felt a rush of superheated anger and roared as he lolloped forwards at full speed, ignoring a storm of laser stars that rained down on him. The XCEL tipped its head as he approached, threw Daisy aside and charged at him.

The white-hot anger inside Darren seemed to boil away every human thought, feeling and memory, leaving only the XCEL and his monstrous rage to fill his mind. Darren roared, rolled and ripped while the XCEL fought back with rapid, blurry slashes and kicks, dipping this way and that to avoid his grapples and punches before launching more blindingly fast laser-sharp attacks, spinning at dizzying speed. Darren was only vaguely aware of the stinging slashes of green light that cut into him as they fought. Neon arcs blurred past him at neck- and waist-height, leaving wound after wound.

Darren's vision began to cloud red, and he instinctively knew his injuries were beginning to drain him. He roared and fought harder, landing punch after punch and kick after kick on the XCEL's metallic torso. But then it started to jump clear of his blows, flipping over him before attacking him again. Darren's reactions were slowing as his human senses began to return. Each hit from the XCEL began to hurt more and a sense of fear stole over him with the realization that he was losing…but he fought on, hoping that every second would help Daisy escape, and using that hope to push away the increasingly real sense that this fight was how his life would end.

Suddenly the XCEL seemed to be slowing too. Darren realized one of its eyes was no longer shining green. He felt a surge of adrenaline, gripping the XCEL's arms as best he could to stop it slashing him while he tried to get a hold around its neck. The XCEL writhed and they rolled as they fought. They were now far away from the trees, moving ever closer towards the Old River Road.

The headlights of an approaching car momentarily distracted Darren, and the XCEL grabbed one of his wrists and threw him. He hit the tarmac of the road and rolled clumsily to his feet. The sound of a horn and screeching brakes filled his ears and he raised an arm to cover his face as the car swerved to avoid him. The roar of the engine was deafening and then the night turned dark again and the sound was receding. The car had missed him by centimetres. He turned to see it skidding sideways and watched in horror as the car rolled down the riverbank, hitting the water with a huge splash before slipping under.

"Darren!" Marek was beckoning. "The SQUID's working." He pointed at the XCEL. "It heals quickly. We don't have much time!"

Darren looked between the XCEL, which was moving towards him, and the spot where the car had been swallowed by the river. There was no sign of the driver surfacing. He pretended for a moment that there was a decision for him to make, but he knew there wasn't.

"Take Daisy," he called to Marek as he began to lollop.

"Oh, for heaven's sake! Hero time, really?" Marek screamed. "Okay, I'm SQUIDing home with or without you!"

"Then go!" Darren shouted, taking a deep breath as he dived into the river.

CHAPTER 21

A FINAL BREATH

Darren plunged into utter blackness and felt the shock of the cold water envelop him, making every wound on his body sting. He ignored the pain and pushed himself down using powerful arm strokes as his eyes adjusted to the murky waters. The front of the car had already hit the riverbed. The mud cloud it had kicked up was being whipped away by the powerful river current, which also pulled at the car boot, threatening to flip the entire car. Darren pushed deeper and let the current drag him towards the car. He flung out a hand as he passed, gripped a roof bar and pulled himself, hand over hand, down to the windscreen. The driver was slumped unconscious on the steering wheel as water seeped in. It wouldn't be long before the water reached her head.

Darren pulled at the driver's door, but the pressure of

the water stopped him from opening it. With nothing to use as a lever, he decided to smash the window to lessen the resistance. He hammered twice with no effect, the water slowing his hand. Then, on his third strike, a crack spread across the glass, the whole window shattered and water poured in. At first the door still wouldn't open, but as more water flowed into the car, it began to budge and then swung out. Darren leaned in, feeling the first pain in his chest from holding his breath. He quickly tore through the seat belt with his hard nails and dragged the driver free of the car.

He swam upwards with one arm around her, willing his breath to last and hoping hers would too. A shimmering moon came into view as they rose clear of the mud cloud, encouraging Darren to keep swimming. Then he saw Daisy wading into the water. With desperate relief, his head breached the surface and he took a huge breath, air rushing into his lungs and clearing his mind. Her face was set in a familiar determined expression as she took the woman from him and started dragging her towards Marek, who was standing on the bank, mini-SQUID in hand. He was waving and shouting.

"IT'S IN THE WATER!" he yelled, looking beyond Darren with an expression of pure fear on his face. Darren turned to see a green light under the surface and only had time for half a deep breath before a hand gripped his ankle and dragged him back into the blackness.

He wrestled the XCEL as they sank, while it gouged at his eyes and tried to twist his neck. The current dragged them down rapidly and slammed them into the side of the car, making Darren release some of his precious breath. He managed to pin both of the XCEL's arms by its sides, and then hooked a leg around the open car door to hold them under water. His lungs began to scream for air, but he held on as the XCEL writhed. He would keep them both down there for as long as possible. For as long as it would take for Daisy to be safe.

The pain in Darren's lungs grew agonizing as the XCEL fought against his bear-hug grip. His thoughts of Daisy turned into memories. Of Daisy, of Mum and Dad. Memories from when he had been very young, before he'd started school. He remembered fun, laughter and a sunny beach where he'd dug a wet sandy hole to hide in all day until the ocean filled it. He wondered to himself, as the pain in his lungs seemed to float away, whether that beach was still as warm and happy a place as it had been then, when he'd been too young to know he was different...

Somewhere beyond the reach of his oxygen-starved brain, one part of his mind was screaming at him. His mouth was open. He was breathing water. He was just seconds from dying. But the larger part of his mind remembered the warm beach and wondered, vaguely, if that was what his heaven would be like.

Then, with no warning, the XCEL went limp. Darren loosened his grip and it simply drifted away, caught by the current, as the green light in its one working eye flickered out. Darren let go of the car as the XCEL disappeared from view. Far away, his brain was screaming at him to swim. He pushed upwards with leaden arms as the pain in his lungs grew even more intense, but everything seemed to be happening more slowly than before. He kept going, trusting that once again he'd see a shimmering moon and Daisy's feet. Then his mouth was open again and water was in his mouth and throat, and the water around him was still a muddy blackness.

"You're Marek, right? Give me your jacket."

"You must be joking!"

"He's freezing. We're lucky he's breathing."

"So?"

"What do you mean, 'so'?"

"This is a Gieves and Hawkes suit!"

"GIVE ME THE JACKET, NOW!"

Darren felt something cover his chest and arms. He vaguely became aware that he was wet and the world was dark, but he could hear Daisy and Marek. It felt like a dream containing two people from different parts of his life who were never supposed to meet.

"Have you got a phone?" Daisy asked.

"Why, do you want to ruin that too?"

"I need to call my parents."

"Is this really the time, Miss Devlin?"

"Well, Mum's a nurse and Dad's a paramedic, so yes!"

There was silence before Marek said quietly, "Is he going to be okay?"

"I don't know."

"Is he going to die?" Marek asked, a surprising trace of uncertainty entering his voice.

"I don't know…" Daisy's voice cracked. "He brought up a lot of water. More than the lady. Check on her, okay?"

"She's still out cold," Marek said. "I can't believe this. It's my fault. He doesn't like it when I get too alien. I let him leave. I thought he wouldn't get far without me, that he'd come back. I underestimated him, just like everyone else. I'm supposed to be cleverer than everyone else!"

"Your phone?"

"What about it?"

"GIVE ME YOUR PHONE!"

"How rude!"

Darren remembered he had a mouth and croaked, "Marek, give her the phone."

"Darren!" Daisy smothered him in a hug. "Oh, Darren!"

"Easy, Daisy. I'm sore."

"Sorry!" she said and leaned away. When he opened his eyes, she was wiping away tears. "You're bleeding!"

Marek loomed over the two of them. "Oh, thank goodness!"

Darren grinned. "Aww, Marek, I didn't know you cared!"

Marek shifted with embarrassment. "I put a lot of time into your outfit. It'd be a shame to have no one to wear it."

Darren started to laugh but was stopped by stabbing pains in his sides. "I think I broke some ribs."

"Stay still," Daisy advised.

"Listen to your sister," Marek agreed. "I don't want you vomiting all over my jacket. Honestly, I ruin a suit every time we go out."

Daisy gave Marek a disapproving look. "Phone?"

Marek handed it over. "Try not to break it," he said, and wandered away to look at the driver, who was lying on her side.

Darren watched him, then painfully lifted himself up into a sitting position. "Is she going to be okay?"

"The driver? I think so. She didn't look as bad as you

when I pulled her out." Daisy looked at him carefully as she waited for her parents to pick up. "Are you okay, Darren?"

"Yeah."

"What was that thing?"

"A killer robot or something."

Daisy tutted when her parents didn't answer and swiped at the phone again. "A robot, seriously?"

"Yeah. The people after us are all machine guns and rocket-launching drones, you know?"

The phone connected and Daisy started speaking. "Mum? It's me. Yes, I know I should be in the house. Mum... Mum... MUM! I need you and Dad to grab your medical bags and some blankets. A car went off Old River Road. Mum... Mum... Stop asking questions and just come, okay? Okay, great. Bye... Love you too... Hurry! Bye."

Daisy ended the call and looked at him meaningfully. "You can't come home, can you?"

Darren shook his head. "Don't see how."

"Then you'd better go before Mum turns up. She'll want to cover you in bubble wrap and hide you in the attic. I'll work on her and Dad." Then she whispered, "Can you trust Marek?"

Darren thought for a while. "I think I have to find out how to."

Daisy bit her lip. "Okay…" She rubbed his arm and then smiled. "I'm proud of you, Tiny."

Darren grinned. "Really?"

"I hate to break up the party, but it would be sensible, *Darren*, for us to go!" Marek called as he walked back to them.

Daisy smiled at Darren. "You know, he's probably right."

Darren sighed. "Yeah, I know."

A familiar voice cut through the night. "That's enough chatting," Miss Inghart said, her tone steely. "I want you both to turn around slowly and kneel."

CHAPTER 22

BE QUIET

Darren spun around and saw Miss Inghart's face break into a cold smile. He felt his anger surge. There she was, holding a gun to the back of Marek's head, the woman who had pretended to be his friend while she turned the world against him. Through all the pain and exhaustion he felt, a deep growl swelled inside him, making his chest rumble. He roared.

Miss Inghart took a step back, looking unnerved, but then gripped Marek around his neck with her free hand and pushed the barrel of her gun harder into the back of his head. "Now, now. Be a good boy, Darren. I want you to kneel down and your sister is going to tie your hands with some cable tie from my pocket. Then we're going to wait while I radio for a helicopter. It'll only take a few minutes. Understand?"

To Darren's surprise, Marek sneered. "Really, Nanny. You want Darren to be 'a good boy'?"

"Quiet, Marek! I've got xenocide in one of these dart chambers. Tranqs in the other. I can take you both down!"

"Quiet? You want me to be quiet, Nanny Inghart? Really, do you? You want me to be a good boy? You always said that, didn't you? 'Be a good boy.' I had to be soooo good for my nanny, while *you* were being a very naughty nanny for years and years, weren't you?"

"I'm warning you, Marek!" Miss Inghart said, and cocked her pistol, ready to fire.

Marek's arms began to flail with anger. "No, Nanny, you don't get to tell me anything! You told me lies for my whole life! I don't even know who my mother is any more! You did that to me!"

"Shut up, Marek!" Miss Inghart snarled.

"Marek!" Darren called. "You just need to be quiet. You need to be really, really quiet!"

Marek didn't answer. Instead, his arms kept flailing. "My whole life is a lie!"

"Marek!" Darren called. "Be *quiet* before the helicopter comes!"

Marek went suddenly limp. He glanced at Darren. "QUIET?"

"Yeah," Darren answered.

Miss Inghart nodded. "Yes, that's right, that's right. Nice and quiet."

Darren watched Miss Inghart smile triumphantly, but then he saw a single marble-like ball fall from Marek's twin-thumbed hand. It rolled back past Marek's foot as it started to grow.

Miss Inghart cried out. The marble was now a rapidly growing sphere around her ankle. The bubble grew and dragged her into the air. She started to point her gun at Marek, but her arm slowed strangely as the bubble continued to expand. Moments later she was struggling in slow motion as the sphere enveloped her completely and drifted away towards the river.

Marek rubbed the back of his head and then smiled. "I feel so much better for getting that off my chest!"

"You all right?" Darren asked.

Marek nodded. "Yes, although a little nervous about this helicopter."

Daisy was looking at Miss Inghart floating away in the expanding sphere. "What is that thing?"

Marek waved a hand. "A proto-universe. It'd take a while to explain properly."

Daisy stared at Marek disbelievingly. "You made a universe?"

Darren pointed at Marek. "He's pretty bright."

"I get that," Daisy answered, still staring at Marek, who looked remarkably smug.

"They can explode rather spectacularly," he explained. "But your brother insists we don't kill anyone—"

"I should hope not!" Daisy interrupted.

Marek shrugged. "As I was saying…we don't kill anyone. Not even my former nanny, who, I have to say, totally deserves it. So if I can have my phone back…thank you, Miss Devlin…I'll make it go pop rather than bang."

Marek tapped his phone and Miss Inghart fell into the river as the sphere immediately evaporated.

Daisy was looking at Marek sceptically. "No explosions? Well, that's a relief." She gave Darren a *Can you believe this guy?* look. He shrugged.

Marek missed the tone in her voice and waved sarcastically at Miss Inghart as she floated out of sight in the fast-flowing river. "That really was tremendously satisfying!"

Darren cocked his head, listening hard.

"What is it?" Daisy asked.

"Mum and Dad's car."

She sighed. "You'd better go."

Darren nodded sadly. "Marek's got a gadget for that."

"Does it make a universe?"

Marek shook his head. "No, just an interdimensional concurrence."

Daisy gave Marek another wary look. "So glad I asked."

"I'll be okay," Darren reassured her.

"Make sure you are," she said, holding both his hands. "Be safe."

Darren swept her into a hug. She gripped him hard and then stepped away as car headlights came into view. "Okay, Tiny, get going."

Marek took out the mini-SQUID and created the swirling disc of colours. "It's been a pleasure, Miss Devlin. When you're ready, Darren. Three mini-SQUID jumps should get us home."

Darren watched the car carrying his mum and dad approaching. "*This* is home," he said, and for a moment he seriously contemplated staying. One moment with them felt worth the risk of ending up in prison or worse. But then he forced himself to think clearly. Too much was at stake now, whether he liked it or not.

He stepped towards the disc and took a final look at Daisy, who was now kneeling by the driver. She curled her right hand into a fist, placed it over her heart and then pointed towards him. He grinned, gave her a thumbs up in return and then walked through the swirling colours, away from Farlington and back towards London.

CHAPTER 23

WHO WE ARE

Darren leaned against the tower railings in Caledonian Park and looked out towards the imposing roof of St Pancras station in the distance. He shoved his hands into his pockets and became lost in his thoughts as he remembered the last time he and Marek had stood there – the last time Marek had asked Darren to join him.

He stretched and ignored the dull ache from the wounds that ten days ago had been agonizingly painful. Marek was sure Darren's monstrous heritage partly explained his rapid healing, but the heavy bruising on his back was still giving him trouble. He'd had no idea at the time just how hard the XCEL had hit him. The memory of it made his skin prickle.

A strange light leaked into the night sky from behind him and he heard Marek's unique footsteps. He turned to see Marek shutting down the repaired SQUID.

"All right?" Darren asked.

"I thought you were going to wait for me."

"I needed some quiet to think."

Marek tutted. "It's been over a week since we got back, during which time we know our enemies have been active, and you've spent more time here 'thinking' than in the bunker." He watched Darren expectantly.

"What?"

"Have you made a decision yet?" Marek asked.

Darren took his time in answering. "Kind of."

Marek smiled. "There's a 'kind of' between 'I'm staying' and 'I'm leaving', is there?"

"Yup."

Marek rubbed his palms together nervously. "Should I assume you have questions? You usually do at moments like this."

Darren didn't look at Marek, but instead addressed his question to the London skyline. "You haven't told me everything, have you?"

"No."

"You knew about XCELs."

"Yes."

"Did you help make them?"

"I invented them," Marek admitted. He looked troubled as Darren turned to stare at him, but he continued. "Nanny

Inghart used to bring me bits of broken technology. It was only towards the end that I knew they were alien. I can only guess that the tech came from that UFO crash at Roswell all those decades ago. I was a child, so I just fixed them or built new things with them and didn't ask questions. Putting Earth and alien tech together was fun. I didn't mean to build a killer cyborg." Marek shrugged his shoulders almost apologetically. "I was eight years old when I invented XCEL technology. I just wanted to upgrade my pet hamster. She was deadly to anything weighing less than five kilograms."

"Your hamster?"

Marek nodded. "Marjorie, my hamster, yes. I miss her, actually. I didn't mean to turn her into a lethal weapon. She ended up taking on a Dobermann guard dog and losing. Anyway, I didn't know they'd be able and willing to make an XCEL out of a human."

Darren looked out at the London skyline again. "You didn't tell me you did things for them, though."

Marek shook his head. "No. I should have done, but you have to understand something: I can think about nine unrelated things at once. I remember everything I've ever seen or read. I understand things no one else can. Every time I open my mouth, I have to choose what not to say. I don't try to mislead you. I just don't know what bits to tell you."

"Because I'm too stupid?"

Marek smiled disarmingly. "Compared to me, Darren, everyone is. Oh, and by the way, I didn't say you were stupid before. I just said you couldn't read. They are totally different."

"They don't sound different."

"But they are," Marek said firmly.

Darren turned to face Marek completely. "Maybe you kept some stuff back because you didn't want me to know?"

Marek raised a hand. "Doesn't everyone? Maybe I wanted you to see, to understand a few things before I started telling you everything. For you to understand Project Helix before I had to admit what I'd been involved in. Before I ran away, they involved me in missions and I made new technology for them, but then I realized Nanny was lying to me. I hate lies. Inaccurate information leads to inaccurate theories. So I *was* going to tell you. I just had to work out when…and how."

Darren stared at him. When he spoke, his voice had a touch of growl in it. "Don't lie to me again, Marek, or leave bits out either."

Marek nodded vigorously. "Darren, I promise."

"Good."

Marek looked hopeful. "So will you come back?

Permanently, I mean? I didn't break the rules after all, did I?"

"Except you almost killed Miss Inghart."

"Well, nobody's perfect. It's just…when I found out my family was all a lie, it surprised me how much it mattered. I didn't consider my family very often, really. I think, deep down, I didn't want to let myself think about them. If I had, I would have guessed it was all invented. It was too convenient. And I hate being tricked. So it's possible I slightly overreacted."

Darren scanned Marek's strange, large-eyed face for every trace of humanity he could find. The eighty-one per cent Marek never mentioned. "Problem is, I still think it'll happen again."

Marek sighed. It was his turn to stare at the skyline. He looked back as he asked, "So where does that leave us?"

Darren stepped closer to him. "We need to be doing this for the same reason."

"And what reason would that be?"

"There were fifty-one kids, right?"

Marek considered the question. "Yes, according to the file I hacked. Project Helix altered fifty-one children, if we include me and you."

"And we're the only ones still alive," Darren said. "Forty-nine died."

Marek frowned. "True."

Darren looked at Marek meaningfully. "We could do this for them."

Marek looked unconvinced. "Take down the organization behind Project Helix for some kids I never even knew? I've always preferred doing things for selfish reasons."

"I know and I don't like that," Darren said, and then pointed at himself and Marek, "but they're inside us, aren't they?"

Marek raised an eyebrow. "If you mean that we have some of the same genetics, then yes."

"Like family."

"Family," Marek repeated, thinking. "Hmm...go on."

"They killed those kids – our family. We can't kill them back. That's like saying our family is just as bad. We're *better*."

"We're the good guys?" Marek asked.

"Yeah!" Darren said hopefully. "Do you see what I mean?"

Marek nodded slowly. "We're doing this for the Helix fifty-one?"

Darren put his hand on Marek's shoulder. "We *are* Helix 51."

Marek thought for a while and then a strange expression stole across his face – the expression of a man trying on a new suit and finding, to his surprise, that it fitted perfectly.

Eventually he pulled out his phone and wrapped his free hand around Darren's shoulder. As Marek prepared to take a selfie, Darren looked at them both on the screen, framed by the night sky. A single beautiful constellation of ten stars was the only thing between their heads. Darren saw a fierce intensity in his own wolfish grin. Marek's smile spoke not only of his usual arrogance, but of a certainty that seemed new. More than that, there was a striking similarity in the determined way they were both holding their chins.

"Very well," Marek said as he took the photo. "From now on, *we* are Helix 51."

EPILOGUE

Councillor Eight poured a large measure of whisky into a crystal glass and studied the view of the Manhattan skyline as she waited for news from Mrs Lahaine. Her mind drifted over the recent disastrous events three thousand miles away in Britain that had ended with the loss of the XCEL prototype. She sipped her drink and sifted through the choices still open to XSP, the Xastris Special Projects division.

She swirled her whisky and turned her attention to three poster-sized photos that were hung, equally spaced, on her office wall under the banner:

XSP's Most Wanted

Each photo was of a young person and had many pieces of string extending from it like a spider's web. Each string led to a photo of a person or name of an organization. The whole web made a diagram that showed everything and everyone that was a part of each teenager's life.

She briefly studied the left-hand photo. A boy stared back at her with a knowing smile. The spiderweb of his life was packed with photos and names you usually only found on the dark web. Under the photo, a label read:

Marek Masters

Location: London, UK

The second photo had a far simpler web. Just a mum and dad, a sister, and one more string that stretched like an umbilical cord to the photo of Marek. The wild-haired boy peered out carefully from the photo with amber-yellow eyes. Underneath, a label read:

Darren Devlin

Location: London, UK

For a moment, she touched the small photo of Daisy Devlin as she considered the events she had set in motion that day, before turning to the final photo. It showed a girl defiantly baring her teeth at the camera. Her pure white hair and eyebrows contrasted with her brown skin. Councillor Eight's neck prickled as she took in the girl's fearsome expression. She scanned the girl's spiderweb, taking in the many photos that were each covered with a red X. Underneath the photo, it read:

Aurora María Ash-Valero

Location: Unknown, USA

She studied the photo for a while longer as she came to a decision, then turned to her desk when a video call came in. Sitting down, she activated the identity-concealment software that all nine Xastris councillors always used, and then spoke in the knowledge that the program would disguise her South Korean accent.

"Report, Mrs Lahaine."

"Ma'am," Mrs Lahaine answered. "If you tune in to the BBC news channel in a minute or so, you'll see the operation was successful."

Councillor Eight smiled. "Excellent. Any problems?"

"None. There were no...unexpected guests," Mrs Lahaine answered. "I assume my next priority is the capture and elimination of Miss Inghart? Mr Ducas will have recovered enough to answer questions soon. We expect he will be able to shed some light on her whereabouts."

Councillor Eight shook her head. "No, I need you to do something else. Miss Inghart can remain AWOL for now. Although she will pay for her incompetence soon enough."

"Yes, ma'am," Mrs Lahaine answered, frowning. "What's the new priority?"

Councillor Eight glanced at the photos on the wall. "Marek Masters must never find out about the other two surviving Helix children. We have seen how dangerous he can be when working with a Helix child, even one as limited as Devlin. We cannot risk him finding another."

Mrs Lahaine was silent for a moment. "I see. There are seven people below gold security clearance level who know the truth."

Councillor Eight drained her glass. "Eliminate them."

"Yes, ma'am."

"No patterns, Mrs Lahaine. If there is any pattern whatsoever in how they die, Masters will spot it."

"Understood. A variety of accidents, sudden illnesses and a mugging gone wrong?"

"That would be perfect," Councillor Eight replied. "No errors this time, Mrs Lahaine." Her tone hardened. "Miss Inghart, after all, is no longer here to take the blame."

Mrs Lahaine took the threat as intended. "I understand. I will organize this personally."

Councillor Eight cut the call and refilled her glass. She dropped three ice cubes in, one at a time, and watched the chaos of overlapping ripples as they plunged into the golden liquid. She switched on her TV and stood again as she watched the BBC news channel with the sound on mute. A breaking news banner read:

Devlin Sister Arrested for Aiding Serious Criminal Fugitive.

The pictures showed Daisy Devlin in handcuffs being pushed into the back of a police car. Her parents stood behind, both in tears, the father holding the mother back as she tried to reach her daughter.

Councillor Eight smiled and turned towards her wall of photos. She raised her glass in a toast to Marek. "Check. Your move."

Marek led the way through the bunker to the Super-SQUID, the truck sized version of his hand-held interdimensional device with the power to reach as far as central Europe. "The XCEL's transmitting again. This is what we've been waiting for!"

Darren felt his skin prickle. "It's alive?" he asked, his mind reliving the eerily smooth movements of the humanoid cyborg that had stalked him through woodland before almost killing him a few months earlier.

"Oh no, don't worry. It's still inactive I'm sure." Marek stopped as they reached the ammo store and turned to look at him. "XSP want it back. Within minutes of it transmitting, their whole communications went dark except around the area the XCEL signal is coming from. I might not know what they're saying, but when they decide to say nothing, it's always significant."

"So, what's with the swimming?"

"Ah, about that…" Marek looked sheepish. "With all our experiments and keeping track of our enemies, I've overlooked a number of modifications I was going to make to my robots."

"Like what?"

"Making them waterproof."

Darren groaned. "You told me that was the only good idea I'd ever had!"

Marek grimaced. "I know! Your words 'what if we end up fighting in a river again?' are ringing in my unreliable ears. I did intend to, but I've been a little busy. I did get this, though." He held up a wetsuit.

Darren took the wetsuit from Marek. "Looks a bit big for you."

Marek smiled. "Sadly, my part-alien bone density, or rather lack of it, means I float rather too well for this situation."

Darren looked at the robots rushing around the Super-SQUID, pulling large tarpaulins across the floor, and remembered the XCEL with an involuntary shiver. "The XCEL's still underwater?"

"Under quite a lot of water, yes."

"How much?"

Marek checked his phone. "About forty metres right now. It seems to be sinking. We should hurry."

Darren was surprised. "That's deep for a river."

"Oh, it isn't in a river. It's floated out to sea. That's why it's transmitting again. Salt water must've got into its communications circuits."

"Which sea?"

'The Atlantic ocean. It's currently off the coast of West Cork, Ireland. Near a place called Schull... I'm not sure how you pronounce that..."

Darren whistled. Something told him swimming out in the Atlantic would be very hard. A flutter of nervousness started in his stomach. "I don't know if I can dive that deep."

"I did intend to see if you could, but I'm fairly sure you'll be fine."

Darren looked at him apprehensively. "Fairly sure?"

Marek made an apologetic gesture with his free hand. "I only have human data to go on but based on that, you'll be able to survive down there for a while…but it is cold, so put this on. I'm told professionals urinate in their wetsuits to warm them up."

"They wee in them?"

"Apparently so."

"Grim. Turn around."

Marek and his robots averted their eyes and lenses while Darren stripped and pulled on the wetsuit. "How do I look?"

"Awful."

"Cheers, Marek."

"You're welcome." He turned to his robots. "Hurry up now! Darren SQUIDs in five minutes!"

As the robots all sped up their work, Darren thought of chilly ocean depths. "How am I actually going to do this?"

"Well, according to the free-diving information I read in the spare few minutes I've had since the XCEL transmitted, the water pressure at that depth means your body needs less oxygen. You can usually hold your breath for at least fifteen minutes. So, you should have longer. Although, if you're swimming hard, you'll use more oxygen, so I actually have absolutely no idea how long you can survive down there."

"Great," Darren muttered as he adjusted the neck of his wetsuit. It was uncomfortably tight.

Marek continued. "On the plus side, the water pressure dissolves so much nitrogen into your blood that you'll become euphoric. So, at least you'll be in a good mood. Now, assuming you find the XCEL, swim slowly to the surface. That is incredibly important."

"Why?"

'Because if you swim up too quickly, all that lovely nitrogen comes back out of your blood as bubbles and kills you. It's called 'the bends' and it's incredibly painful."

"Slow. Right."

"Until you're about ten metres down. Then you might want to hurry up."

Darren sighed. "Do I want to know why?"

"Because at about ten metres below the surface, the water pressure lessens and you suddenly need more oxygen again. It means you can black out and drown."

Darren thought for a minute. "So... You don't know

how long I can stay deep before I drown. And if I come up too quick, I drown, and if I come up too slow, I almost get back and then drown?"

Marek nodded. "Yes, I'm glad you followed all that. To be perfectly honest, this is more dangerous than when you fought the XCEL in the river –" he waved a hand – "but you usually work these things out, so I'm sure you'll be fine."

"Question."

Marek sighed. "You usually have one or two."

"Why don't I use an air tank?"

"An aqualung? Sadly, I don't think you can."

"Why not?"

"Those incredible lungs of yours. A normal human only exchanges about ten or fifteen per cent of the air in their lungs in one breath. You are more like a sea mammal. You can exchange fifty to sixty per cent of the air in a single breath. That's why you can hold your breath for so long. The problem is an aqualung breathing apparatus isn't designed for that. Depending on the design, my best guess is you'd either feel like you were breathing through a tiny straw when you inhale, or you'd breathe in so much compressed air that getting the bends would be a certainty. I'd have to redesign a special one for you and we don't have time."

"Right. So, I take a big breath, dive down…'

Marek interrupted. "No, the currents will make it almost

impossible for you to find the XCEL if you dive down. Underwater, I can estimate its position to within about twenty metres. I'll SQUID you in under the water. Then you swim to it, grab the XCEL, swim up slowly…"

"You can't SQUID me back from down there?"

Marek shook his head solemnly. "No. I'd have to leave the SQUID portal open while you find it and swim through. At that pressure, a huge amount of sea water would come through in a high-pressure jet. The entire bunker would be flooded and, frankly, I don't see any reason to put my life in danger."

Darren gave Marek an appraising stare. "Glad you've got your priorities straight."

"Pleased you agree!"

Darren adjusted the cuffs on his wetsuit which were pinching his skin. "So, I swim up and then what?"

"Hopefully, I'll be able to lock on to your position and SQUID you back." Marek threw Darren a pair of goggles.

Darren caught them. "I don't need these. I can see underwater."

"They can follow the XCEL signal. The direction it is in will look brighter than the rest of the water. That's all I could manage in the time."

Darren put on the goggles while Marek's robots retreated from the ammo store. Looking at the huge tarpaulins,

Darren realized Marek expected a large amount of seawater to come splashing through even in the fraction of a second the Super-SQUID would be open to put him in the middle of the Atlantic Ocean. He turned to look at Marek and realized he was wearing Wellington boots with his usual snappy suit.

"Nice boots."

Marek's eyes narrowed. "We shall never speak of them again!"

Darren grinned and then thought through everything Marek had said. The dangers seemed immense. "We really need the XCEL, don't we?"

Marek nodded furiously. "We really do. This could well be our best chance of stopping the people behind Project Helix."

"I'll get in the Super-SQUID, then."

"Excellent. I'll see you in a while…hopefully… It'll be fine. Fun even!" Marek grinned with excitement and then retreated.

Darren climbed into the Super-SQUID. "Marek?"

"Yes?" Marek's voice crackled over the comm.

"What's the weather like out there?"

"Why?"

"If there's big waves, are you going to able to SQUID me back?"

"Just a minute… Ah, yes… Hmmm… The winds are gale force 8 and rising."

"Is that bad?"

"It's basically edging towards a sea storm. So, yes, SQUIDing you back might be a little…tricky?"

Darren rubbed a hand through his hair. "Right."

"There's a rock with a lighthouse called Fastnet nearby. Swim for that if I can't SQUID you back."

The knots in Darren's stomach intensified. "Alright."

"Oh and look out for our old friends. They are bound to be up to something. I've been doing my best to interfere with their communications."

Darren's nerves mixed with a strange sense of relief. He was finally actually doing something. "Okay, let's do this."

"Take a deep breath."

Darren took a huge breath. A split second later, a swirl of colours appeared around him and he was gone.

WILL DARREN RETRIEVE THE XCEL?
AND IF HE DOES, WHAT SECRETS
WILL IT REVEAL ABOUT XSP?

FIND OUT IN
21% MONSTER: ICE GIANT
COMING JANUARY 2023

DISCUSSION QUESTIONS

WARNING: CONTAINS SPOILERS

1. *"Everyone wants to make Darren a problem and focus on what's different about him, but he deserves more than that."* Consider the judgements people make about Darren. How might his life change if those differences were not seen as a "problem".

2. Darren is unable to read and write. What impact does this have on Darren and his day-to-day life? Think about shopping, travelling, going online etc.

3. On p48, Marek reacts strongly to Darren referring to himself as a freak, saying; *"I'd prefer you didn't use that particular word. That word is for fools who don't understand the power of being different. Who don't realize that if all people were as similar as they'd like them to be, the human race would have died out just like the dodo."* Is Marek right? How do genetic differences benefit the human race?

4. Marek mentions the 1947 Roswell incident on p49 and

p274 as the possible source of his alien DNA. Why do you think the author decided to link his fictional work with a historical event shrouded in conspiracy theories?

5. What ideas about aliens and monsters in stories and culture do you think inspired Darren and Marek's differences and abilities?

6. You have the technology and resources to create a gadget which could help Darren and Marek battle Miss Inghart and Ducas. What does it do, what it is called, and can you come up with a clever acronym for it, like the SQUID, the QUIET bombs or the CLAM?

7. In justifying his behaviour, Marek tells Darren, *"We're not human, Darren. To them we're not quite human, so why should we obey their rules?"* Do you agree with Marek that he and Darren are *"not human"*? What does it mean to be human?

8. Look at the conversation Devina, Grant and Robbie have about how to engage with Darren on p134. Do you think they do the right thing?

9. Marek is unable to hear or appreciate music. How

might this make someone's life significantly different? Think about the last film you watched or the last party you went to.

10. You can be either 21% monster or 19% alien; which would you choose, and why? If you could be genetically modified using the DNA of another species, what would it be?

11. Why did the author choose 19% and 21%? How might Marek and Darren have been different if the percentage was higher or lower?

12. Robbie risks his job by giving Darren a lift, but says "*one day, someone will need help and you'll be able to help them... That's how you make things right, okay?*" Do you agree? What one thing can you do today to help someone?

13. The book ends with Marek and Darren acknowledging that their shared genetics with the children of the Helix51 experiment means they are "*like family*". Discuss the theme of family in the book. Look at the Epilogue again. Can you predict how this theme might take on more significance in book two?

USBORNE QUICKLINKS

WOULD YOU LIKE TO FIND OUT ABOUT THE SCIENCE BEHIND SOME OF THE IDEAS IN THIS BOOK?

At Usborne Quicklinks we have provided links to websites where you can:

- Find out about genetics, the study of genes and DNA.
- Zoom into a human cell to look at DNA, genes and more.
- Make a 3-D model of DNA.
- Find out how to extract DNA from fruit and vegetables, with the help of an adult.
- Try a test-yourself quiz about genetics.

To visit these sites, go to usborne.com/Quicklinks and type in the title of this book.

Please follow the internet safety guidelines at Usborne Quicklinks. Children should be supervised online.

Thank you for reading this book. I hope you enjoyed meeting Darren, Marek and Daisy. I *really* enjoyed writing about them! They first popped into my head about ten years before I wrote the book. It took me a long time to find a story that suited them, but once I did they took charge and decided where the plot would go. I just followed. Writing is a lot of fun when that happens.

In case you've been wondering, viruses really can leave DNA behind after they make someone ill and there are also animals who are a mix of two different species. They are called hybrids. So, an evil organisation creating someone like Darren with a synthetic virus is more possible than you might think.

As for Marek, I had to make a few assumptions about the alien who provided nineteen per cent of his genetics because I've never met an alien, even though I'm sure they are out there – somewhere. Working out what an alien might be like was a lot of fun. However, this is the first book in a series so I won't reveal too much about that or some other interesting characters you'll meet if you keep on reading. Some of my favourites are still to come! What I will do is promise that there are more adventures in wait for Darren and Marek and some surprising people for them to meet. Daisy has some tough times ahead and important friendships to make. Miss Inghart and Mr Ducas are going to get some close attention from someone very powerful and extremely dangerous, and Marek will get the opportunity to use some more *brilliant* gadgets. I hope you'll join me for those stories because Darren may need all the support he can get to save the world...

ABOUT THE AUTHOR

P. J. Canning has a PhD in Chemistry and now lives and works in Cambridgeshire. His scientific background has influenced the backdrop of *21% Monster*, lending the series a satisfying authenticity and logic. He is married with three children – all of whom are brutal critics of his work. Peter once heard someone say, "write about what you know", but he thought writing about monsters and aliens would be much more fun. *21% Monster* is his first novel.

ACKNOWLEDGEMENTS

I have quite a few people I would like to thank, both for their help on this book and for their support more generally. So, please do go make a cup of tea and get comfortable before continuing.

First of all, I have to thank my agent, John Lomas-Bullivant for spotting something in this story. After twenty-three years of rejections, having someone so engaged and willing to creatively challenge my work from so early on made a massive difference to my writing. Thanks also to Sue Cook, Ingrid Selberg and Annie Eaton who provided expert advice in the early stages of this book's journey to publication.

I was then incredibly lucky to work with my editor, Stephanie King, whose positivity, creativity and insight have been hugely influential on this story. Usborne is a very special publisher who have a genuine enthusiam and respect for children's publishing. I am lucky to be one of their authors and to have worked with a fantastic group of professionals, including Anne Finnis, Jacob Dow, Kat Jovanovic, Jess Feichtlbauer, Sarah Stewart, Gareth Collinson, Becky Walker, Alice Moloney, Sarah Cronin and finally designer Will Steele who took Coke Navarro's fantastic illustration and turned it into a remarkable cover. Throughout, they have all been dedicated in working to make *21% Monster* as good as it could possibly be. Thank you all.

I would also like to thank some fellow stunningly talented authors who have been supportive during this time – Clare Povey, David Owen, Cat Gray and G. M. Linton. Their advice and sympathy has been invaluable.

But of course, writing is only ever part of a person's life. My wife, Michelle, has put up with an author as a husband and I thank her for that and all the other ways she supports me from the bottom of my heart. I would also like to apologise to my children Gemma, Sophie and Eoin for the inconvenience of having a children's writer as a father. Their willingness to be a captive audience to test out ideas has had a huge influence on this book. Your love and support means everything to me. You are all so special!

I'm lucky to have always had the backing of my parents, brother and sisters, and also to be part of a large family of nieces, nephews and in-laws, all of whom have been amazingly excited that this book is finally hitting the shelves. I thank and love you all.

Of course, there are others – friends and colleagues past and present who have given me strength and moments of laughter in so many ways. Some have or are trying to write books themselves. Others are pursuing other dreams. I thank you, and I hope you all keep chasing. Dreams are not always caught, but the pursuit can make gods of us nonetheless.